AF414964

# SAVAGE BEAR'S FATED MATE

## MISTY VALE SHIFTERS 2

### SAMANTHA LEAL

BOOKS IN THE MISTY VALE
SHIFTERS SERIES


Dragon Daddy's Nanny (Book 1)
Savage Bear's Fated Mate (Book 2)

Savage Bear's Fated Mate

Copyright ©2021 by Samantha Leal

All rights reserved. No part of this book may be reproduced in any form or by any electronic of mechanical means, including information storage and retrieval systems, without written permission from the author, except for the use of brief quotations in a book review. The unauthorized reproduction or distribution of this copyrighted work is illegal. No part of this book may be scanned, uploaded or distributed via the Internet or any other means, electronic or print, without the author's permission.

https://www.totallyromancebooks.com/samantha-leal

Join the Totally Romance Facebook Group!

# CONTENTS

# CHAPTER 1

The drive into the mountains was quickly turning into a treacherous one. Stella braced herself by gripping the wheel tightly and squinting her eyes as the fog kept descending, making her wonder whether she could even go any farther.

"Yikes," she breathed out, her sigh showing her exactly how cold it was inside her car. Her breath produced a white blast in front of her. She reached forward and turned up the heat. It wasn't even winter, but as she headed north, she could sense the distinct chill in the air and knew that she was heading home.

She was heading back to Misty Vale after all this time…

It was something she had never thought she would ever do, and yet, here she was, making the journey after being gone for so many years. She didn't know much, but she knew that it was certainly going to be interesting after she had fled an entire decade ago. The memory of it all was still hot and fresh in her mind; it never truly left her for a second. *How could I ever forget the sorrow that haunted me all those years ago?* she considered. Stella had left her adopted hometown to start somewhere new the moment she had turned sixteen, and now that she finally had the courage to go back and face her demons, she wasn't going to let any amount of fog or cold stop her. She just had to be strong.

She thought of her last memory of the place she had called home ever since she had lost her parents in a tragic accident when she was just a child invaded her mind. She knew it was a quaint place; one that was charming and rustic, with its small-town appeal, but she had never immersed herself in it; not fully. She had been so withdrawn and nervous, after her parents' death, that she had hidden away at home for most of her youth, shying away from friendships and only truly having her eccentric aunt for company. She had always yearned to be back in a city, to try to regain some semblance of the life she had lost, so she packed her bags as soon as she hit sixteen and headed out into the world on her own.

She was lucky that her aunt had been understanding and had visited her often, but now, it was her turn. And she was doing it in epic style. She wouldn't just be going for a visit; instead, she had packed up her life and was going to try again in Misty Vale. This time, she was going to give it a real chance. *City life is only fun in your early twenties, and I am creeping closer to thirty.* She wanted stability. *And the cost of living in the city, and the price of purchasing a home; I really want to own something of my own, and soon. And I think it is about time I settle down and have some sort of family around me. My aunt is all I have, she considered.* Even if it did terrify her when she thought about letting people get close to her after losing the most important people in her life, it was hard for her to let go.

She cranked up the radio and tapped the wheel. She only had around fifty miles left to go, and she was winding up and around the mountain roads in the final stretch, just hoping the fog would keep at bay a little longer and not get too thick. The last thing anyone wanted was to be stranded out there in the cold, after dark, with the thickest fog she possibly had ever seen.

"Here we go, Stella," she half-smiled to herself. "This place is already trying to throw challenges your way, but you know you've got this."

She slowed her pace as another bend came up ahead of her, and she was almost engulfed in a thick cloud of fog for a moment, before it cleared, somewhat, again, and she could see. It really was becoming ghastly out there, but she wouldn't be defeated. Not now, not yet...

As the roads became narrower, and she began to feel the familiar shape of the twists and turns, she knew that she was getting ever closer, and soon, the roads would flatten out and widen, and she would be on the last part of her journey, and back into a life she had run from all those years before. *Just a little farther, you can do this. Slow and steady, Julia.*

She pressed her foot to the gas and sang along to the music, when, all of a sudden, her car let out an almighty bang and she felt the wheel begin to shudder within her grip.

"What the...?" she gasped as she pressed the brake and slowly came to a stop. The fog was still around her, but she could clearly see from her headlights, reflecting off the fog, that smoke was coming from under the hood.

"Oh, hell no..." she whispered to herself. "This is not good."

She looked around her out of instinct, but the fog was now starting to make it truly difficult to see the rest of the road. She took a deep breath and pressed the gas again, the car juddered as if it were struggling as she made her way a little higher and out of the main density of the mist. She could see a little clearer, but before she had the chance to pull to the side of the road and out of the way of potential oncoming traffic, her car ground to a painstaking halt. The engine seemed to splutter and then it went quiet.

"Oh man…," Stella said, putting her head in her hands. "You could not make this up."

After being so sure and confident and ready for anything, it seemed as if the world was against her tonight… And now, she was indeed stranded on the side of a mountain, in the middle of a very cold haze, her car packed full of bags, and the remainder of her things still in the city. And she would bet her life that she didn't have any signal on her cellphone either. *Because why would I have signal. After all, it is* Defeat all Attempts for Julia to Get Home Day, *right?*

She turned the key and completely shut off the engine, but left the lights on, before she stepped out of the car and made her way off the road, with her phone gripped tightly in her fist.

She stopped when she was safely away from the road and looked back at her car. She hadn't seen another vehicle out here for what could easily have been an hour, but she wanted to be safe. She looked at her phone and tapped it to life to see what she had been dreading but hadn't truthfully known.

She had no bars. No service. No way of contacting help.

She winced, bringing it back down and sliding it into her pocket. Now, she was going to have to either walk around the mountain and hope that she got signal somewhere… or wait in the cold dark until someone drove along. She stomped her foot in frustration and grimaced. Could this honestly be going any worse?

"Sure, back to Misty Vale after all this time? What could possibly go wrong?" she said aloud as she held out her arms and stared up at the night sky as if she were searching for answers.

"Come on, though, give me a break!"

And at the exact moment she said it, she heard the distant

rumble of a car engine and the sound of music along with it. She grinned and made her way back toward her car, just hoping and praying that whoever was heading this way was paying close attention to the road and wasn't about to plough into her car headfirst.

She gritted her teeth and waited for the oncoming crash, but as the car got closer, she saw the headlights appear through the fog and it was clearly not as thick as it had been before. It was a truck, and it slowed right down before pulling off on the other side of the road and shutting off its engine.

Stella clapped her hands together and looked up at the stars.

"Thank you," she whispered.

The truck door opened, and she looked on as a figure emerged from the driver's side. It was a man, alone; one dressed in dark jeans, a thick sweater and a leather jacket. He squinted as he searched for her, looking past the headlights of her car and into the darkness beyond.

"Hey, there," he said, his voice deep and gruff but also appealing. It was a strong voice, a masculine voice, one that would have gotten her attention whether she had been stranded on a mountainside in the cold, dark night, or crossing a busy street in the middle of the day. There was something about it that held power and presence.

*I like it.*

"Hi," she said as she stepped forward and raised her hand in a wave.

And as she got closer, and their eyes met, she felt something happen inside of her. She felt a gear shift, a change of balance, something big and unbridled that she had never felt before in her life, just by really looking at another person. Her mouth sagged slightly as he took another step closer and his features came fully into focus; his incredible dark eyes, the way his hair was wavy and pushed back off his face in a perfect curl, the dark stubble on his chin and the way he carried himself so strong and confident.

*My, oh, my…* she thought. But then she had to stop herself from swooning, from showing how clearly attracted to him she was because he had stopped to help her; she was in no position to be lusting after anyone in this moment. She was totally screwed and needed his help!

"Are you okay?" he asked as he put his big hands on the hood of her car before stepping back and cringed. "This car does not look good," he said as he took in the smoke still trailing up from under the hood.

"It just gave up on me," she said, holding out her hands. "I don't know what I would have done if you hadn't stopped, thanks so much."

He looked unsure for a moment, and then glanced back at his truck as if he hadn't intended on sticking around. He looked back to her, his eyes wide and engulfing, but his head clearly leading him in another direction. He looked back to his truck and then down to her.

"I… I was going to…," he began but then sighed and stopped, and then shook his head.

She glared at him, not willing to take no for an answer, and she could tell that he sensed that in her.

"Let me take a look," he said with a friendly smile. "Nothing quite like a damsel in distress to change your plans…"

She smiled shyly, and he winked, and she was pretty sure that, somewhere between them, a fire had started burning.

# CHAPTER 2

*S*mith Savage hadn't intended on leaving town on the week that Oktoberfest was due to begin, but sometimes, life just throws curveballs that can't be missed, no matter how hard you may try. As a bear shifter from one of the founding families of Misty Vale, Smith had always had his fair share of responsibility and stress. But with tension rising between the bear and dragon packs, and the recent arrival of a lawless biker gang, he was finding it hard to get fully involved in the usual proceedings of Oktoberfest… And it was beginning to take its toll. He needed a break, and he wanted to get out of Misty Vale while he had the chance, but it looked like it wasn't meant to be.

Now, here he was, his truck stopped on the side of the mountain, only twenty minutes out of town, his plans completely capsized by what could end up being the biggest curveball of all.

This damsel in distress.

The girl with the large, beautiful eyes and fiery demeanor.

He knew the second he was in her presence that he was

fucked. His bear came raging to the surface, his instinct was going wild with something he had never met before and he was going to have to do his best not to give in.

*Surely, this couldn't be it?* But everything was telling him it was.

He had wanted to leave town, he had needed the escape, but there was no way he could leave her out here in the foggy darkness. No way at all. Not this girl.

She was watching him over his shoulder, and he breathed in her scent. She was different, he had known it the second he laid eyes on her when she had stepped out of the shadows cast by the headlights, but now that she was even closer to him, he worried.

*Was she part dragon? Or something similar?*

Smith couldn't be sure, and that wasn't like him. He was usually on point when it came to figuring out both humans and shifters alike, but this girl was a mystery. All he did know was that she had his attention, and he was feeling something that unnerved him. Something that appealed both to his bear and to his heart. It felt as if she was it. *The one.* The mate he had been waiting for and the one that he was going to be determined to resist, no matter how hard his bear was going to fight to claim her. It was throwing him off his game and he didn't know where to look or what to say. His instinct was to protect her, to sweep her up and put her in his truck, drive her back to town and ravage her... claim her. He had not been prepared and he was going to have to stay strong. This could not happen, not now.

He frowned and tried to focus his attention on the smoking engine in front of him. This was a mess. There was no way he was going to be able to fix it there and then.

He probed further into the mechanics and knew that this girl was not going to be getting the car back on the road any time soon. He looked up at her and could see the reflection of the stars above in her eyes. They twinkled, and it made him smile warmly.

"Well," he said with a wry smile. "I'd say this is completely caput."

She closed her eyes and winced.

"I thought as much," she moaned.

He closed the hood and they both leaned back on it. The fog was beginning to clear, only now revealing their position high on a mountain turn. For this vantage point, Smith could see the road for a few miles in either direction as it hugged the mountains. Although he couldn't see any cars at the moment, that could change quickly. They were in no immediate danger of being ploughed into, but he had to get the car off the road quickly before their luck changed.

"I'll move it," he said. "I should be able to roll it off the road, but I don't have any tow equipment with me."

"What can we do?" she asked hopefully.

"Well..." he paused. "I could come back out tomorrow and take it to the closest town, which is Misty Vale..." he trailed off.

"That's perfect," she grinned. "Because that's exactly where I'm heading."

He raised his eyebrows. That hadn't been what he was expecting, but he supposed Oktoberfest was about to begin, and she was likely a tourist.

"Oh really?" he asked with a wry smile. "You in town for Oktoberfest?"

She looked at him as if she didn't know what he was talking about, and it made him even more intrigued.

"No," she smiled. "I'm moving back there... it's kind of my hometown."

Now, she really was making his mind go wild. He had

never seen this girl before, and now, she was trying to tell him that Misty Vale was her hometown?

"Mine too," he said as he cocked his head to the side. "I'm pretty sure I've never seen you around before."

"Well, that's because I've been far away for a very, very long time…" she said with mystery and a hint of teasing as she raised her own eyebrow and laughed.

He laughed too. This girl was a bit of an enigma. She was devastatingly stunning in her beauty, she seemed full of fire and wit, and she was easy to be around. Now, she was making him smile and laugh… *Boy, am I in trouble.* His bear was yearning to be closer to her, to know more, and there was a tingle raging its way down his skin from the top of his head to the tip of his toes, making him feel as if something were being awakened in him.

He had to be strong and resist. It was unnerving.

They kept looking at each other for a moment, as if they were trying to figure each other out, and then, Smith finally stood and pulled a pair of gloves out of his pocket.

"Okay," he said. "If you get inside, take off the brake and leave it in neutral, I'll push from behind. Do you think you'll be able to steer it off the road?"

When he asked the question, he realized how stupid it must sound. She had managed to drive all the way out here… It was clear she was perfectly capable.

"Yeah," she said with a smirk. "I know I'm the damsel in distress, but I'm sure I can manage that one."

He flashed her a smile and nodded in defeat before he moved around to the back of the car and waited for her to climb inside. As he watched her and the way she slipped behind the wheel, he had the feeling, again, that she was something a little different… something that he couldn't quite put his finger on.

It almost seemed like fate that she should be out there, blocking his exit from Misty Vale on a night like tonight.

His bear was standing at full attention… His urge to claim her was strong, but his heart battled to stop him. Now, he just had to find out why.

# CHAPTER 3

*S*tella looked at Smith as he drove them toward Misty Vale. This certainly had been a night quite like no other. She couldn't believe her journey back to town had been thrown so many complications, but she had to admit, she was kind of glad this one had happened.

She didn't know what to make of Smith yet... He was aloof and seemed to find her both amusing and curious. She saw the way his eyes widened slightly when she spoke, the way he seemed to be sizing her up as if he wasn't sure what to make of her either. But she knew he was hot as hell, and for that reason, she wasn't going to rule him out just yet.

As they approached the town, and she saw the sign come into view, a ton of memories began to flood her mind. She saw the town's crest welcoming them, and it made her sigh. The dueling dragon and bear, fighting over a crown... *How could I ever have forgotten it?* It seemed to be printed everywhere at one point when she had been growing up. It was on her high school sweater, on some of the old stores that had run along Main Street, and now, as she was returning, it had been the first thing to jog her back into what it had felt like to be a resident all those years ago. The familiarity was in some ways reassuring, but at the same time she hoped that perhaps other things would be different.

She had been so lonely as a teen, shying away from any social interaction outside of school hours. She had longed to get away from here, from the heartache she seemed to associate with this place, but now, as she was coming back as an adult, with a ton of life experience, she was relieved to know she didn't feel as overwhelmed with emotion as she had feared. In fact, dare she admit, she was a little excited?

She saw the lights shining brightly down from the Grand Lodge high up on the mountain, and as they pulled onto Main Street, she smiled as she recognized a couple of the old places from her youth, but also because she saw that this place had most certainly moved on for the better.

"So," Smith said as he cast his glance over to her. "Where are you heading?"

She looked at the time and knew there was no way her aunt would still be at work, but part of her wanted to see the store all the same. She had heard so much about it; she had poured over email pictures and it had been part of the reason she had agreed to come home. It looked so magical and fun; a place Stella could imagine bringing her back to life.

"Well," she said. "I guess I better get to my aunt's place."

"If you need anything, we can stop somewhere here on Main Street," Smith asked.

She smiled. It was like he had read her mind.

"Are you sure?" she asked, hopeful. "I would only be a moment."

"Of course," he laughed. "Hell, we've come this far."

Stella chuckled. She liked this guy, and she was already feeling far too comfortable in his company.

She nodded and smiled, and so, he pulled to the side of the road and parked. She could see the lights shining out of

Treasured Sweets up ahead, and all the baby pinks and blue bursting out in color from the window display, mixed in with some of the fall accents that her aunt had already told her they would be changing up this week to a full-on Fall and Halloween display, ready for the season.

"I'll be right back," she said as she unclipped her seatbelt and opened the car door.

She walked quickly to the front of the store and felt a rush of happiness to finally be seeing it in person. Apart from the window display, it was rather dark inside, but she could still see plenty of the shelves and the old sweet jars that were lined up around the outside of the room. It looked idyllic, like a traditional candy store that she used to visit on vacation as a child, and she clapped her hands together with excitement as she felt a rush of pride. Her aunt had created something truly special for Misty Vale, and Stella felt honored to be a part of it, even if it was in just a small way.

She turned back toward the street, having to tear herself away from it before she practically beat down the door with excitement, and jogged back to the truck to see Smith waiting.

She felt a flutter in her belly as she climbed back inside and looked up to him and his bemused expression.

"So, do you just really like candy stores or what?" he asked with amusement.

Stella laughed and shook her head.

"You seem intent on teasing me," she said.

He shrugged his broad shoulders as if she had been asking for it, and it made her laugh even more.

"It's my aunt's place," she said as explanation. "I haven't been back to town since it opened and I'm excited to see it. I'm going to be working there and helping her out."

She saw his head tilt to the side, and he looked at her with even more interest. She felt as if the moment she had laid eyes on this guy, it was almost as if they had known each other. But she knew she had never laid eyes on him before… It was deeper than that. As if their souls were speaking to each other, making connections their eyes and mouths at that moment could not.

"You're Camille's niece?" he asked.

She didn't know why she was surprised to learn that he had heard of her. But she had to remind herself, this was not a big city that was full of strangers. It was Misty Vale, and clearly, Smith and her aunt had crossed paths, at some point. Especially, with her running one of the stores on Main Street.

"Yes," she smiled. "How do you know her?"

Smith started the engine and smiled, but there was something behind it, as if he were now a little concerned.

"Well, mainly, because of her running the store, and you know… Small town life." He laughed.

"Yeah, I guess," Stella said.

"But also, my family and I are the ones who organize the Oktoberfest… and Camille has been providing refreshments and running a couple of stalls since it began."

"Oh really?" Stella asked with intrigue, the penny beginning to drop for what this might mean going forward.

"Yeah." Smith laughed as he made his way out of Main Street and in the direction of Camille's house. "So, I guess that means we're going to be working together and seeing a lot more of each other…"

Stella tried not to smile too wide.

"I guess so," she said as she looked out the window, away from him, and bit her lip.

*Misty Vale…* she thought. *What wild plans are you going to throw at me next?*

* * *

When Smith pulled his truck onto Camille's street, Stella breathed out deeply as more memories came flooding back to her. Her aunt had not moved, and her house stood proudly at the end of a small cul-de-sac, one that had been improved a lot over the years. All the houses had been well-maintained and the paint was all fresh, making them look as if they could have just been built recently, but still retaining their more historic charm. Camille's was looking out at them, with lights lit in the windows and a cozy vibe seeping out from beyond.

"Well," Stella said as she looked to Smith. "I have to say, thank you so much. I don't know what I would have done without you tonight."

"It's no problem," he smiled, his eyes open and his expression warm.

She still felt the pull toward him, as if she could easily reach out and take hold of his hand, but she stopped herself and smiled meekly.

"I'll get my things put into the truck and head out at first light to tow your car back to town," he said. "My family has a garage just off Main Street. Your aunt will know the one. I'll take it there and get them to have a look at it for you."

"Thank you," she said, genuinely humbled by how kind he was being to her. "Are you sure? You've already gone to so much trouble."

"Of course, I'm sure," he half-laughed. "I have a feeling that meeting you, tonight, may have saved me from making a terrible mistake."

She watched the way he looked out the window, as if he were suddenly deep in thought. She had no idea what he meant, but she was glad that she had helped all the same.

"Well, thank you again, Smith." She smiled as she reached for the door handle, her body yearning to stay close to him.

Smith opened his too, snapping himself out of his

moment of deep concentration, and headed around to the back of the truck to help with some of her bags.

As she walked toward the house, she couldn't help but look over her shoulder, her mind racing and her heart thumping. He was so hot, had been so kind to her, and now that she knew she had a reason to see him again, it made her all the more excited.

"Good night, Stella," he called to her, and she turned to face him fully from the steps of her aunt's porch, and she smiled and waved.

She could see the glint in his eye and could tell that he was feeling it too. It was powerful and had the potential to knock her off her feet. She took a deep breath before she turned and tried to compose herself. She was going to have to get a grip. She couldn't be feeling like that about a guy when she had just rolled into town. Plus, she had an innate fear of getting too close to people and had the habit of pushing them away. None of this made sense and she was going to have to try and get a hold of herself.

She heard his engine start, and she made a point of not looking back again; instead, she reached up and knocked loudly on her aunt's door. She had barely rapped her knuckles on the wood when it came flying open and her Aunt Camille was rushing at her, throwing her arms around her and pulling her in tightly for a hug.

"Oh, Stella," she said with sheer joy and delight. "You're home."

She held her aunt tightly and felt genuinely pleased to be there. It had been so very long since she had set foot in this house, and yet, when she opened her eyes and looked past her aunt and inside, it was as if she had never been away. It was all so familiar and all so welcoming that it actually felt good to be there.

Her aunt helped take her bags and ushered her inside.

From out on the street, she heard Smith's truck disappearing into the distance, and she couldn't help but think of him again too, wishing she'd had more time with him but also knowing she would soon see him again. So much had happened in the past few hours that her head was in a total spin, but she had made it back to Misty Vale, and she had made it back to her aunt's.

"Come on through." Camille beamed as she took hold of Stella's hand and led her into the back of the house where her cozy kitchen was waiting, smelling delicious and of freshly baked cookies.

"You're so late," Camille said as she pulled out a chair and ushered Stella to sit down. "But even so, I couldn't resist making your favorite."

Stella clapped her hands together, like a giddy, excited child and grinned up at her aunt.

"This is like stepping back in time," she laughed. "But I love it."

"I'm so glad you're here," her aunt smiled. "But where the devil have you been? I was expecting you no later than nine and it's almost eleven o'clock."

"Oh, have I got a story for you..." Stella said with wide eyes. "I take it you didn't notice I'm not in my car?"

Camille shook her head and grimaced.

"I got stuck on the mountain; it just conked out on me. But luckily, a very handsome and kind man came to my rescue. He gave me a lift back here and is going to head back out in the morning and tow the car back to a garage for me. I don't know what I would have done without him; he totally saved my ass."

Stella laughed, and she saw her aunt's eyes shine with warmth too.

"I'm so glad you're all right," Camille said, holding her hand up to her chest. "I've been stuck on the mountain before too, and I wouldn't wish it on anyone, especially at night."

"My phone didn't have any signal, so I have no idea what I would have done if he hadn't come by. He was like my knight in shining armor." When Stella said the words, she didn't realize how dreamy she had made them sound, as if she had already fallen head over heels. It wasn't until she looked back to her aunt and saw the suspicious look on her face.

"Oh really?" Camille asked knowingly, with a raised brow. "And who might this knight in shining armor have been?"

"…Smith," Stella said with a grin and after a long pause. "I didn't catch his surname. He knows you, though."

Camille's eyes widened slightly, and she sat back in her chair.

"Smith Savage?" she asked, her expression changing from one of intrigue to one of concern.

"I don't know…" Stella said warily. "I just know his family runs the Oktoberfest and they own a car garage in town."

Camille nodded her head slowly, as if something was clicking into place.

"Oh yes, that's Smith Savage all right," she said with a half-laugh. "A nice man… but not one you should be mixing with."

Stella furrowed her brow.

"What do you mean?" she asked, her heart beginning to sink.

"Smith…" Camille said ominously. "Well, Stella… He's a *bear.*"

And just like that, Stella's heart truly sank to the pit of her stomach. All the memories and politics of Misty Vale rapidly began hitting her hard all over again.

*Welcome home, Stella,* she thought. *Welcome home.*

# CHAPTER 4

With Stella's car firmly attached to the tow rope and bar at the back of his truck, Smith was already heading back to town with it before the Town Hall clock had even struck 7am.

He had barely slept all night, tossing and turning, constantly churning over the events of the past day, but also the run up to Oktoberfest. It had been a stressful few months, and it had culminated in him wanting to leave town without even telling the rest of his pack. They had driven him mad over the course of the past year, and he felt the tension in town rising between the bear and dragon shifters. It was surely only a matter of time before something kicked off, and Smith had not wanted to be there to witness it.

But then, last night had happened. He had thrown a bag into the back of his truck, jumped behind the wheel, and headed off into the night. *What sort of cruel twist of fate was it that Stella had been there, broken down in the midst of the fog and the dark, blocking my path and in need of saving?*

He had felt something instantly with her, and he knew something important was happening, but he was also wary.

Even if every instinct in his entire being was telling him to claim her, he had to hold back.

She wasn't just any girl.

This was Stella, the niece of Camille. A cousin of the infamous Striker and Dash Livingstone, two of the most powerful dragons in Misty Vale. He knew that they had family that weren't shifters themselves, and he sensed something different in Stella the moment they met. And now, he knew why. Even though she wasn't a shifter, she had been touched by dragon magic... And he wondered which one of her parents had been closely associated with the dragon clan, or indeed had been born into them.

He knew Camille well, and she was the same as Stella, touched by dragon magic but not possessing it herself. She had regularly spoken of her niece who lived away, so for Stella to return to town and come bursting straight into Smith's life, it all seemed so crazy.

But Smith had plenty of reasons to not get involved with anyone involved with the dragon clan. The age-old bear – dragon war was only just the tip of the iceberg. Smith had never trusted the dragons, and when his last girlfriend had run off with one, leaving him with a broken heart a few years ago, he had sworn that he would never mix with them again.

*But... Stella...*

Stunning Stella, innocent and vulnerable, out on the mountain. Someone whose soul had spoken to him in so many ways, just by one look. She had stirred something inside of him that he had never felt before... And yet, now, he learned she had come from a dragon family, even if she wasn't a dragon shifter herself or had dragon's blood flowing through her veins.

He sighed as he turned down Main Street and tapped his fingers on the top of the wheel.

He felt conflicted and in a right mess.

He hadn't been looking for this, and yet, he hadn't been able to stop thinking about her since the moment he had met her. She had haunted him all night, and he had laid awake, staring up at the ceiling, remembering how his skin had felt on fire when their eyes had met. How his bear had growled deep inside of him, wanting to break free.

*Stella.*

*How could someone so innocent and pure be affiliated with the dragons? Why would fate do this to me?*

It had caught him completely off guard.

But he was glad for it, all the same. Now, he hadn't left town on a whim, he had been brought back by her, and no one in his pack had to know that he had thought about leaving. He knew, deep down, that he couldn't run from responsibility; it had just been a mad moment. So, he had Stella to thank for that. She had brought him back to where he truly belonged.

He pulled behind Main Street and into the parking lot of the garage, before stopping and turning the key. He could see that his brother-in-arms, Brandon, was already inside, working on another vehicle, and had, no doubt, been there since the crack of dawn. He waited for Brandon to look up from underneath the hood and then he waved before getting out of the truck.

"Morning, Brandon," he called. "How's it going?"

"Well, this is early for you," Brandon laughed, rubbing his hands on an old rag. "What's going on?"

He approached slowly and craned his neck to see around the back of the truck to Stella's car waiting there, attached by the rope.

"I helped a girl out on the mountain last night," Smith said. "She had broken down, said it just crashed out on her. I saw smoke coming from the hood and took a quick look, but it looked as if it's going to need some serious repairs."

"Lucky for her, you were going by," Brandon said. "Well, if you detach it, we can push it into the shop, and I'll take a look when I get a chance."

"Thanks, bro," Smith said as they both slapped their hands against each other's and then came together for a hug. "I don't think there's any rush on it. She seems to be back in town for a while."

"Who is it?" Brandon asked.

"Some girl called Stella," Smith said, and when he said her name aloud again, it felt good. Something just for him. "She's Camille's niece."

"Oh, really," Brandon said. "Interesting."

"Well, I guess we'll be seeing a lot of new faces in town in the next few weeks with the festival starting up," Smith said, trying not to allude to the fact that Stella was, in any way, of interest to him. He knew what his bear brothers would think, and he wasn't in the mood for a lecture.

"Yeah," Brandon laughed. "Things sure are about to get crazy."

"Yeah," Smith shook his head. "I always hate this time of year… and I know, I'm a terrible example of community spirit."

He winked, and Brandon laughed. Their clan may have been the organizers, but that didn't mean they always had to enjoy it and thrive on it, especially with how things were feeling in town at the moment.

"Thanks for taking a look at that for me," Smith said as he began to step back and undo the tow rope. "I appreciate it."

"No problem," Brandon said with a shrug. "I'll let you know how it goes."

"I told her it would be here, but I'll drop by and tell her you're dealing with it, if I get chance."

Brandon nodded, and he and Brandon prepared to push the car into the shop.

It had been an early but productive start to the day.

* * *

ONCE THE CAR WAS SAFELY TUCKED AWAY IN THE SHOP AT Brandon's Mechanics, Smith drove back onto Main Street and pulled up outside one of the cafes. He was starving and had done nothing but think about either Stella or food that morning. He walked into his favorite place for breakfast and ordered the biggest bacon, egg and cheese bagel he could get his hands on. He could see that the town was already filling up with new faces, and Main Street and their stores were already beginning to sell German-inspired delicacies. He smiled when he saw Bratwurst on the menu, and with the rumbling in his belly, admitted defeat and ordered one of those too. He was going to have to get into the Oktoberfest spirit, and he felt himself relax as he collected his food from the server and stepped back outside.

Misty Vale was his home.

*What was I thinking, wanting to leave?*

He thought back to Stella and of what it must have taken for her to pack up and leave all those years ago. She certainly was brave, and he couldn't help but wonder what else was going on with her. Her Aunt Camille may have mentioned her, but he had never heard anything about her parents or any siblings. And if Misty Vale was Stella's hometown, then how come he didn't know who they were?

The plot was beginning to thicken, and as he drove back to his cabin in the woods, having to stop himself from instantly ripping into the bagel, having some self-control until he was home, he thought on it some more. He wondered who this girl was, and why his bear was so drawn to her. How he had done nothing but yearn for her since he had left her outside Camille's the night before, and how, now, he was turning it over in his mind about calling her, when, deep down, he knew that he shouldn't. It was torture to know that she was staying at Camille's house and that the number was sitting there in his cellphone.

"No," he said aloud as he swung the truck onto his make-shift gravel driveway in the middle of the forest. "You've got other things to be focusing on. You can't let your head get turned by a woman."

But he felt as if he already knew his denial was futile.

Stella was already getting into his bones. And it was shaking him to his very core.

He opened his front door and stepped inside his rustic cabin, smiling as he took it all in. He had built the cabin, from the ground up, with his bear clan brothers, many years ago, and it had expanded over the years, evolving into something truly special. It was perched in the depths of the forest, surrounded by some of the most incredible views, and it was quiet and idyllic, away from the rest of the town, but close enough to walk to, if he ever had one too many beers at Archer's Bar in the evening. Smith loved being amongst nature, and the bear in him loved the forest. It was where he felt most at home, and as he kicked off his work boots and wandered through to the kitchen and out the back door, onto the veranda, he took in the view of the pines and the mountains, and breathed in the fresh air.

He did love it here.

He sat down on his favorite outdoor chair and ate his breakfast, savoring each bite. And by the time he had finished, he couldn't believe that it was only just creeping toward 9am.

He had waited and waited, and now, he couldn't any longer. He was going to call Camille's house and speak to Stella to get it out of the way. And then, he was going to do his best to not think about her again. He had to be strong.

She was part of the dragon family, and no good could come from him falling for her or pursuing her. He was going to have to put common sense forward and stick to it. Even if his heart was tugging him in another direction.

He rose to his feet and made his way back inside and toward the phone hanging up on the wall.

This was definitely the best thing for him to do…

He just had to see it through and not cave on anything else.

# CHAPTER 5

Stella looked at the familiar framed photographs that ran along the wall of the staircase in Camille's house and smiled. She saw memories of her as a child, sitting in the center of town on her aunt's knee, some of her in her high school graduation gown, and more recent images of her aunt visiting her in the city after she had fled Misty Vale. The girl in the graduation photographs looked broken and unhappy, and she was a complete stranger now. She couldn't believe that she had ever existed like that, and she had come such a long way since. She smiled and reached up to adjust the frame slightly. She felt sorry for that version of herself, obviously still so deeply scarred by the loss of her parents, but she had overcome so many challenges and she was a completely different person now. She had grown, she had thrived, and now, she felt ready to set down her roots back in this town and make something of herself here.

Her first night had been a pleasant one in her old bedroom. After she had left, her aunt had completely stripped and redecorated it, at Stella's request, So, although it was familiar in some ways, it wasn't like stepping back in time. She had slept well, and when she had woken to a bright morning and showered, she felt like a completely new woman. The only thing that was niggling at her wasn't the dreadful memories of her parents' loss but of Smith and the way he had turned up in the fog and saved her the night before. She smiled when she thought of him; he made her feel warm inside, and she was eager to speak with him again and hope that her car was now safe with whichever mechanic he had mentioned.

But her Aunt Camille had most certainly thrown a spinner into the works and made her question everything. Smith Savage… He was a shifter bear. And she knew what that would mean. Her family was in the dragon line, and although she had been able to forget all about the drama and politics of this place when she had left Misty Vale, it seemed like nothing had changed, and she was going to be pulled right back in.

It was still so crazy to comprehend, that there were magic beings that lived in this town. That there were men who could turn into dragons and bears, that there was a vampire that kept himself hidden away and an ancient Fae girl who had been in the town for decades but had barely ever aged. When her aunt had first started opening up to Stella about all of these things when she was bordering on becoming a teenager, she had just taken it as fantasy, but as she had continued to grow and learn, she had realized there was a lot more than meets the eye. Her cousins, Striker and Dash, they were powerful dragon shifters, and she had always felt protected by them and under their wing when she had been growing up. It was another reason she had felt self-conscious at times, as if she should shy away. Not only was she overcoming a life-changing loss, but now she had two cousins who were fucking dragons to contend with and live up to. They had been kind to her, but she knew they would hate it if she ever went outside their clan and dated a shifter bear.

Stella didn't know a whole lot about their ancient feud, but her aunt had already filled her in that things were tense again at the moment, and she knew that wasn't going to be good. When two powerful supernatural entities begin to fight with each other, a whole different kind of insanity could be unleashed, not just on Misty Vale, but on the entire continent. And it was a terrifying prospect.

She looked at the photographs on the wall again and sighed. She came from one messed up mix of a family, but she was older and wiser, and most certainly strong enough to cope with whatever was thrown at her now. Even if it did mean she would be keeping Smith at arm's length and hoping that she didn't let her head get any further pulled in his direction.

"Good morning!" Camille beamed as Stella stepped into the kitchen and breathed in the fresh aroma of coffee.

There was something that was instantly better about everything when her aunt either cooked or brewed, and to smell the fresh coffee brought her right back into feeling warm and yummy.

She sat at the table, and Camille brought over a pot and a mug before pouring some for her and joining her.

"How did you sleep?" she asked.

"Wonderful," Stella said with a stretch. "It was so nice to be back here. I had been worried it would stir up old memories, but so far so good."

Camille smiled and rested her hand on top of Stella's.

"You went through a lot when you first came to live here with me," she said reassuringly. "But I can see the change in you. You're a grown woman, now, who has lived out in the world alone, and I can see you're at ease."

"I am," Stella smiled. "I didn't know how it was going to

go, but being back here now, it almost seems like I never should have been away."

Camille smiled and then took hold of her coffee, blew the steam from the top and took a sip.

"Well, I never, in a million years, thought I would ever hear that…"

"I need to find Smith somehow and ask about my car," Stella said.

She noticed her aunt instantly stiffen, but she didn't say a word.

"Do you know where I might find him?" Stella knew she was pulling the lion's tail by asking, but she just couldn't help herself. Her aunt surely couldn't care that much if she struck up a friendship with Smith… She wasn't a dragon shifter either, she was just from the same family as Stella was.

"Well," Camille said eventually, after a long pause. "He has various businesses around Main Street, I'm sure you'll bump into him at some point."

"But I kind of want to speak to him today," Stella laughed. "For all I know, he could have forgotten, and my car is still stranded on the side of a mountain somewhere."

"I'm sure he hasn't forgotten, Stella," her aunt smiled warmly.

"But what if he has?" Stella heard the frustrated edge in her voice, and she could tell Camille had picked up on it too.

"The bears tend to hang around in the sports bar on Main Street," Camille said reluctantly. "Archer's, I believe it's called."

"Okay…" Stella said with a warm smile. "Thank you."

She wanted to roll her eyes but refrained. *Why couldn't she have just said that in the first place?* She didn't understand why her aunt was being so difficult. Clearly, she was not thrilled about Smith, for whatever reason. Even though Stella had decided to be good and not encourage him, her aunt's resistance kind of made her want to.

Being told 'no' rarely made someone listen or want to comply.

She sipped her coffee and stared into space, thinking of where the sports bar was and if she could remember passing it by, when the phone began ringing.

She gasped and jumped, almost spilling her coffee, but she instinctively rose to her feet before her aunt had the chance to go first and she picked up the receiver.

"Hello?" she said cheerily down the line.

There was a brief pause, and she just knew.

It was him.

"Hello, Stella?" Smith's voice came drifting down the airwaves to her, and it made her heart beat harder and her whole body swoon.

"Hi," she said coyly, turning so her body was angled away from Camille and facing out toward the kitchen window.

"It's Smith," he said, even though they both clearly knew that he didn't need to.

"I know," she smiled and bit her lip. "How are you?"

"I'm good," he said, gruffly clearing his voice and snapping her a little out of her daydream of speaking to him and hearing him speak again. "I just wanted to let you know that your car is safely at Brandon's Mechanics. I headed out and towed it at first light. He's going to check it all over when he gets a chance, but I can't imagine it will be for a couple of days. He's swamped over there."

"That's okay," she said. "Not to worry, I'm not in any rush for it back. And thank you so much..." she said, wanting to say something more but completely unsure of what.

"Hey, it's no problem," he said warmly.

She smiled, and a silence began to build between them, which she didn't like or want. She could feel her Aunt

Camille's eyes burning into the back of her head, and it was making her act out of sorts, as if she couldn't just relax and chat to him how she normally would if she were on her own. She bit her lip again, willing herself to find something to say, and fast.

"Will I see you there?" she finally blurted, instantly cringing and closing her eyes, wanting the ground to open and swallow her whole.

What was that? Why on earth would he be there when he had just called to tell her he'd dropped it off?

"I erm…" he began. "I've left it in Brandon's capable hands…"

The tension between them was alive and well, and she wished Camille hadn't been standing right there watching her, so she didn't feel like such an idiot.

"Oktoberfest starts tomorrow," Smith said, breaking the uneasy pause. "You should head down and check it out."

"Oh, I will," she smiled. "In fact, I think I might be working with my Aunt Camille, anyhow…" He trailed off as she cast a glance back to Camille, who returned her a curt smile.

"Well, that's great," he said cheerily. "I'm sure I'll be seeing you down there."

"Okay, Smith." She felt satisfied, as if she knew where he would be and that she just had to get off the phone before she said anything else dumb. "Thanks for letting me know about the car."

"No problem, Stella…" he said, and then she heard the line quietly click.

She hung the receiver back in the cradle and looked back to her aunt.

Camille cast her eyes down to the table and picked up her coffee, as if she were trying to pretend that she hadn't just been listening and sizing up their conversation. Not that there had been anything to size up there. Just Stella making herself sound silly.

"Don't panic," Stella said teasingly. "I'm not going to run off and get corrupted by a bear just yet..." she winked. "He was just calling to let me know he had towed my car and it's with the mechanic in town."

"Well, that's certainly very kind of him," Camille agreed, before she rose to her feet and went over to the sink. "I suppose I better be getting down to the store, if you want to come with me?"

"I'd love to!" Stella beamed. "I can't wait to see it properly and in person."

"I've been getting everything ready for the Oktoberfest for a few weeks now," she said. "I have things for the stalls packed up and ready to go, and plenty of stock to replenish the shop with the oncoming onslaught of activity, visitors and tourists."

"Looks like I picked a good week to come back," Stella said with a wry smile. "Lots going on and plenty of people to meet... It'll feel like a completely new town to me this time."

"It certainly will, dear." Camille smiled as she reached up and pulled Stella in for a warm hug. "My, it's so good to have you here."

"It feels good to be home," Stella agreed.

*Home.*

It had been some time since she had ever referred to Misty Vale as that...

# CHAPTER 6

The mountain was cold and the ground underneath their paws was hard and welcomingly cool. As Smith and his pack roamed through the pines, he felt the power of his bear surge through him, driving him forward and making him yearn even harder for the woman he couldn't possess.

He looked up at the moon, noting the fullness of it and the way it lit up the earth around him. It looked magical out there, and the town was on the verge of something so big and powerful that he felt it in his bones.

One of the bears nudged him and growled, and he turned to see that it was Archer. He nudged him back, and they began to jump and knock into each other, both of them wanting to burn off the remaining steam they had before heading back to town and into the fray. They had a big night ahead of them and shifting as a pack was just the beginning.

Smith bumped into Archer and rose onto his hind legs before he went back onto all fours and began to chase him down the side of the mountain, snapping at his heels before they both tumbled into the forest.

His energy was raging, and he felt good, the bear-blood coursing through his veins made him feel revived. But he also felt different. Something had changed within him; he wasn't the same bear he had been the last time he had gone to shift. His heart felt different, as if there was more weight to it, more substance; his fur and skin beneath it prickled and he felt as if it were alive with someone else. A pulse of some-one... And he knew exactly who.

*It was Stella.*

He had never been stirred like this, and his bear knew it. It was trying to tell him, trying to warn him of what was about to come. But instead of fearing it, Smith was eager to explore it. He knew, now, that it wasn't something he could resist.

*Stella. My fated mate.*

He looked up at the moon breaking through the gap in the pines and roared. He would embrace his destiny.

He felt good, powerful, alive... and now, he had purpose too.

* * *

ARCHER'S BAR WAS POSITIONED IN THE CENTER OF MAIN Street and had been a total success since the moment it had opened, five years ago. Smith and the rest of his pack were heading there after their shift on the mountain, and he had been looking forward to this since his escape from Misty Vale had been fatefully stopped by Stella.

It was the night before Oktoberfest began, and he and his pack members traditionally came together to celebrate the start and to kick off the proceedings in true bear fashion.

As he walked into the bar, he looked around and could see that it was already busier than normal. The town was bustling, and he noticed the new and unfamiliar faces sitting in booths or playing pool in the game area. He sat up at the bar and ordered a beer and whiskey chaser, before he cast his eyes back to the door, expecting to see some of his pack members walking inside, instead, seeing the bikers.

The Forsaken Riders.

He raised his eyebrows, and they nodded at him. For a small town such as this, it had been an interesting development when a bunch of lawless bikers had rolled in to discuss business. But they had come to the bear pack and they had shown interest in Oktoberfest. Now, the bikers and the bears had been in discussion as to how they could expand their own business empires… But it hadn't gone unnoticed by the dragons. And Smith was very aware of the tension beginning to rise all over again and cause a shift in energy in Misty Vale.

There had been a feud between the bears and the dragons for decades, but as the years had slipped by, the exact cause of it all seemed to have become twisted and lost. He remembered his grandfather telling him stories when he was a child, but since he had been fully in his power, his pack and the dragons had remained on okay terms. They had coexisted without any real problems, until lately. And it was beginning to make everyone nervous.

Smith turned back to stare at the screen above the bar and at the sport. He had never been a huge fan of anything competitive, preferring to focus on issues that actually affected the world at large.

He took a swig of his beer and again felt a rush of longing for Stella. It hit him out of nowhere and his senses were suddenly on high alert. It was as if he could feel her inside of him, as if he knew she was near, and it made him feel even more alive.

He felt the heat pulse through him, the tension in his own bones rise, and when he realized the rest of his pack was coming into the bar and starting to sit around him, all he could hear was the thump of his own heart. He couldn't shake himself out of it, it was as if he were being called somewhere else. He sniffed the air, wondering if he could catch her scent. But he couldn't. He could feel her so strongly that he barely even registered when Brandon put a protective arm around his shoulder and started to ruffle his hair.

"What the fuck?" was the first thing he heard over his own heartbeat as he started to come back into the land of the living. "What's going on here; you in some kind of trance?"

Smith shuddered and blinked, and when he looked up to see Brandon, Archer, and the rest of his pack members looking back at him with both amusement and confusion, he couldn't think of anything to say. It was as if all he could do was just look at them blankly.

"You were somewhere else just then," Archer said as he put both hands on his shoulders and looked at him deeply in the eyes. "Earth to Smith? Do you read me?"

The pack roared with laughter, and Smith smiled and managed to laugh a little too… But there was something unsettling and frightening about it. As if his soul had been lost for a moment, looking for Stella above the airwaves.

The bears all settled in at the bar and began to order drinks, sink beers and chat about the fact that, once again, they had pulled together a great festival for their town. The proceedings would be kicking off at noon the next day, with a selection of traditional bands in the center of where all of the beer tents had been set up, and morale was high. The night before it all bean was always one of the bear packs' favorite nights of the year, and it made everything seem worth it, after months of stress and planning.

The bears acknowledged the bikers, who were now beginning to filter across the room to join them, and Smith felt himself relax. He had been so full of tension, and then everything had happened with him trying to leave town and accidentally meeting Stella, that he felt as if he had been doing nothing but overthinking ever since.

When the door opened, a cold blast of air came with it; he felt the rush on the wind, and it stilled him again.

His bear instinct stood to attention and kicked in with full force. He knew it was her... He sensed her like he had earlier, but this time, he caught her delicious scent too, and it stunned him into stillness.

When he looked up and watched her walk through the door with her aunt by her side, he felt his mouth instantly curl into a smile. But his body was feeling something even more overpowering... He felt so drawn to her, so completely taken by her, that he knew, there and then, that there was no way he was going to be able to resist what was happening. No matter how much adversity may come their way.

*Stella.*

The woman who had stolen his heart.

He was beginning to realize that there was more to all of this than he ever could have imagined, and he was so happy that she had arrived.

# CHAPTER 7

Walking into Archer's Bar wasn't as nerve-racking as Stella had expected. She had managed to twist her aunt's arm about heading out for a celebratory drink after a successful day at Treasured Sweets, seeing what it was truly all about and doing the final preparations for the beginning of the festival in the morning.

Camille hadn't been overtly keen, but in the end, she had agreed. And with Stella knowing that Smith and his other bear friends liked to hang around in Archers, there was no way she wasn't going to aim for there to see what it was all about.

From the outside, it looked unassuming and well put together. It was fashioned to look traditional in style, with wooden frontage and potted pine trees flanking the red double doors. It had a special seating area, walled in with planters that ran either side of the building out front, and it looked well-patronized. From the outside, Stella could hear the loud voices, the music, and the cheers for the football game that was no doubt playing on the TV. It was good to see so many tables filled outside as well, with people wrapped up warm, drinking both beer and hot drinks in mugs.

"This looks great," she had said to her aunt before they had stepped inside, and Camille had nodded.

"It's a popular spot, that's for sure," she said.

As they walked inside, and Stella saw how fun and full it was, she felt a great energy rocket through her body. At first, she thought it must just be because she was being swept up in the atmosphere, but after a couple of seconds, she realized it was much more than that.

She could feel Smith. She felt his eyes on her; she felt his particular energy; and she couldn't help but smile, a rosy blush spreading across her cheeks. The crowd was big and surging, and she noticed there was a large group of men at the long main bar, cheering with each other, doing a shot of whiskey and then all slamming their glasses down onto the mahogany.

She knew he was there, and it didn't take long for him to slowly turn, and for their eyes to lock. All before she had even taken two proper steps over the threshold. It was all so powerful and strong, and as her eyes focused in on his, she felt something inside of her click into place.

Seeing him again was reaffirming to her the way she knew she had felt since the second she had met him. He was someone important, even if it did terrify her.

Camille seemed to sense the connection across the room, and she reached out and touched Stella gently on the arm to steer her toward the opposite end of the bar. As they walked, Stella couldn't help but glance toward Smith again and give him a coy smile. She could see his attention was fully on her, and that it was clear that he was feeling something too. But at the same time as Camille leaned in to speak to the bartender and order them a bottle of red wine, Smith was swept up in a big crowd of his bear brothers and they began to move to the other side of the building toward the game area.

"Smith is over there," Stella said, just to state the obvious to Camille.

"Oh, is he?" she asked, non plussed.

Stella had to really try not to roll her eyes, and even though she knew that her aunt was just being protective and trying to guide her in the best direction, she couldn't help but feel irritated by the fact that she was as well. Surely, Camille would want Stella to find a real reason to stay in Misty Vale? Why try to block her from making a genuine connection just because Smith was a goddam bear shifter?

*This place and its dumb rules*, she thought.

Camille handed Stella two empty wine glasses and they headed to a booth on the opposite side of the building from where Smith and the other bears had gone charging. They sat down, and Camille poured them the wine, and they held their glasses together and said cheers.

"To your first day back in town," Camille beamed. "It's so good to have you back, darling."

"I'm glad to be back," Stella said, finding herself instinctively looking for Smith across the crowded room. She had the feeling she would be doing a lot of that, now that they were both in the same airspace and she could feel his presence.

"Treasured Sweets is incredible," Stella smiled. "I know you've sent me pictures over the years since it opened but seeing it in person took my breath away. What a magical place for Misty Vale, and especially at this time of year with the holidays approaching and a festive air running through everything. The kids that live here or pass through with their parents must love it."

"And the adults alike," Camille winked. "You'd be

surprised at how much it can ignite magic in a grown-up too… I mean, look at you right now."

"That's true," Stella laughed. "When we walked in there, earlier today, I felt as if I were back in some kind of dreamland fairytale."

"That's what I wanted to create," Camille nodded approvingly.

The store truly was amazing. It was two floors with a spiral staircase; rows upon rows of candy and traditionally styled sweets lined the walls in jars. Camille had also started to sell stuffed toys, so the big displays made the whole atmosphere of the place even more magical, and it was certainly a hit with both the residents of town and the tourists.

They had spent the day exploring each part of the store, and then they had chatted about Oktoberfest and the fact that it was beginning the next day. Camille and Stella had agreed that Stella would man the store while Camille did the stall down in the main part of the festival, which was guaranteed to be busier on the first day. Camille had always run the store on her own with the help of a Saturday girl, but now that Stella was back in town, they were going to be splitting the hours and managing the place together.

"Do you think I'll be okay in the store tomorrow?" Stella asked tentatively.

"Sure, you will," Camille laughed. "You've worked in stores before and know how to use the cash register. I think the majority of business we get tomorrow and over the weekend will be down near the beer tents where the market is set up, but I can always have someone on standby to come help you if it starts to get out of hand."

Stella was relieved to hear this; she hadn't fancied the thought of spending the whole day on her own if the store suddenly started to see an influx in footfall. She didn't understand how it couldn't; it was a great spot in the middle of Main Street and the town was already bustling with people. While they had been in the store all day, plenty of people had been in and out, and they had done many sales. It was so good for Stella to quickly learn the ropes on how things were done.

She sipped her wine and felt herself begin to relax. While she had been back, she hadn't yet seen anyone that she thought she recognized from her past, but that didn't mean there wasn't anyone from high school in the bar at that moment. It made her wonder if she would even know who they were now. It wasn't as if she had gone out of her way to make friends back then, and she wasn't going to hunt anyone out for company now.

"I wonder if anyone recognizes me," Stella half-laughed as she thought on it. "I don't know why, but I thought I would walk back into Misty Vale and it would be just like it was ten years ago. I'm so glad it's moved on and is nothing like the past."

"This place has changed more than you know," Camille said with a raised brow. "The whole town has improved. So much is happening here, and the industry is booming, both tourism and property alike."

"I remember it being sleepy, as if I couldn't breathe here… Now, it's completely different. I actually feel like I kind of belong here."

Camille smiled, but Stella noticed her eyes flit to the side of the building where the bears were playing pool, sinking beer, and generally being loud and obnoxious. She could still see the concern etched behind her gaze, as if she wanted to say something but knew it wasn't her place.

"You do belong here," Camille said eventually. "Your family history began here… Even if not your direct bloodline."

Stella remembered the dragon magic she had been touched with, and it made her want to wince. There were so many politics when it came to existing in a place like this, where there had been bad feelings and feuds rumbling away for over a hundred years.

"What's the deal with the bears then?" she asked, feeling brave after her wine glass was almost empty and she was reaching for a refill. "Do the dragons still hate them with a passion?"

Camille laughed and shrugged.

"I try to stay out of all of that," she said. "But, obviously, I'm aware that there is tension, and I don't want you getting caught up in the crossfire by mixing with…you know…*Smith Savage.*"

Hearing his name again sent a shiver down her spine, and it was impossible for her not to smile. Her aunt must have seen how warm and giddy she appeared because she crossed her arms over her chest and pouted.

"I'm a grown woman," Stella reminded her. "But I appreciate your concern." Stella smirked and then shook her head with amusement.

"I know, dear, I know," she said. "I just want to do right by…" She went to say something but stopped herself, and Stella knew instantly what that something was, and she bowed her head and had to look away.

*Her parents.*

Camille wanted to do right by Stella's parents.

Stella felt herself bristle. She knew her aunt's heart was in the right place, but her parents hadn't been dragon shifters, and Stella wasn't one either. They just had family that were. So, really, it all felt a little over the top to be trying to police her in such a way, and now, just vaguely tiptoeing around her parents and their untimely death was making Stella feel guilty.

"It's okay," Stella said. "You don't have to say anything else."

She took another swig of her drink but noticed Camille hadn't refilled her own.

"I'm tired," Camille said. "How about we call it a night?"

Stella flicked her eyes around the room; it wasn't even late, and they still had half a bottle of wine on the table. She was feeling like she wanted to party and didn't really care that she had to be up for her new job in Treasured Sweets in the morning.

"I think I'll stick around here for a while," she said. "But I won't be late."

Camille didn't protest. She just leaned in and gave her a hug before she pulled on her coat and headed for the door.

Stella watched her leave and then she breathed out deeply, letting the warmth from the wine seep through her veins and closed her eyes for a moment to allow herself to truly relax. What a time it had been for her and coming back here was certainly not only interesting but also bringing up fresh challenges. The feud had been something she had long forgotten about, and now, suddenly, she seemed on the cusp of it. It was bizarre.

She had only been sitting alone for a matter of moments when she noticed that the bear crew was all stirring up lots of noise and attention. They were so loud, cheering and drinking, playing pool and, clearly, all in competition with each other. She found herself smiling, and, obviously, looking for Smith, but she couldn't find him in the crowd and felt a sinking disappointment.

She picked up her wine glass and took a long, deep gulp.

"They're not always so rowdy," the voice came from over her shoulder, and she nearly jumped out of her skin.

She turned her head slightly to look as Smith stepped forward from where he had approached and moved in front of her on the other side of the booth, leaning against the wooden railing and looking down at her with a mischievous smile.

"Jeez," she said, laughing and holding her hand against her heart. "You almost scared me half to death!"

Smith laughed, and she couldn't help but take in how hot he was. He was wearing old blue jeans, a black t-shirt that was tight and clung to his muscly torso, his thick, rock-hard arms peeking out of the sleeves and fully catching her attention.

*Wow*, she thought. *Imagine the power behind those arms.*

And she wasn't thinking of how he had pushed her broken-down car off the road. She was thinking of something much, much naughtier. She bit her lip and grinned, wondering if he knew what she was thinking.

"Where's Aunt Camille?" he asked mischievously, a knowing smile spreading across his lips.

Stella rolled her eyes jokingly and then leaned a little across the table.

"She's gone home," she smiled.

The wine was making her feel more relaxed and confident, and she could see the same echoed in him. As if he had been waiting to unwind like this all day.

She couldn't help but wonder if he had been thinking of her too and had been hoping to see her around town tonight.

"I don't think she likes me much," Smith said with a grin. "Am I right?"

Stella smirked and raised her eyebrows.

"I don't think it's you, in particular..." She let the sentence hang between them, and then she shrugged, hoping he would catch on that she knew about him; about the bears, and the long-standing feud that was allegedly about to rear its ugly head.

"Ah," he said, before he raised his beer bottle to his lips and took a swig. "I see."

Stella nodded.

"Join me," she said, motioning to the empty side of the booth.

Smith wavered for a moment, as if he was unsure, but it was so fleeting, she barely even noticed it.

"I hope she doesn't come back and kick my ass," he said with obvious sarcasm.

"I'm sure you'll be fine," Stella laughed.

Smith laughed too, and then he leaned across the table slightly and looked at her, his eyes wide open and engulfing. She felt stilled for a moment, and she smiled back, her heart beginning to pound harder in her chest. She felt him all over every inch of her, and she wanted to speak, but her mind was completely empty, just focused on him and the way his presence affected her in such a profound way.

"I thought about you a lot today," Smith said, breaking the silence. "I know I shouldn't be saying it… But I can't help it."

"I don't see why you shouldn't be saying it," Stella immediately corrected him. "Their feud isn't ours."

He smiled and nodded knowingly, as if he were glad that there wasn't anything that he was going to have to explain. He could tell she knew all about the shifters of Misty Vale, and what he was, and what her family ties could mean for that.

"Maybe we should sneak out," he said with a wry smile. "Before anyone catches us talking."

Stella laughed, but she wasn't against the idea. In fact, she couldn't think of anything better.

She rose to her feet without saying a word and pulled on her coat, slipping the half-empty bottle of wine into its big pocket and raising her finger to her lips to say, *"Shh, don't tell."*

Smith raised his eyebrows in approval and stood up too, doing the same with his beer, but leaving it poke out the back pocket of his jeans. As they wandered toward the door, Stella was sure she heard some of the bears calling for him, asking where he was going, but he put his hand on the base of her back and they kept moving, neither of them looking back and both of them grinning from ear to ear.

They snuck out into the night and began to walk.

This was already the most fun she'd had in years.

# CHAPTER 8

Sneaking out of Archer's Bar with Stella turned out to be quite a thrill.

They laughed as they started to walk away quickly, and Smith watched as Stella dipped her hand into her pocket and pulled out the wine bottle before bringing it to her lips.

She looked so stunning beneath all the twinkling lights that had been lit for Oktoberfest, and as they passed under the big sign that had been hung across Main Street, Smith had a great idea.

"I know," he said as he pointed toward the park and the area where the festival had been set up. "Why don't we go check it out in advance. I can give you a sneak preview?"

Stella looked at him and nodded, her eyes wide and expectant.

"I'd love to see it after all I've heard about it," she beamed. "Plus, getting a secret tour ahead of time makes me feel pretty special."

"Oh, trust me, you are," Smith laughed. "My pack and I have been very guarded, this year, about letting people on-site. You are a very, very important guest."

She dipped her shoulder in jest as if she knew that already, and Smith laughed again. He reached down and slipped his hand into hers, grasping her palm with his, and it made his whole body swoon. To feel his heat against her skin, to feel the connection of their two bodies, it was something completely surreal. He felt as if just being close to her, their hands connected, was bringing them more intimate by the second, as if something big was forging between them. Something so powerful that it was going to be impossible to break.

They wandered off Main Street and didn't say a word. His hand felt electric in hers, and he could tell that something was happening to her. He felt his energy morph into hers, and it was stunning her into silence. He knew he wasn't imagining it; it was as if he could feel what she was feeling. He could feel that he was somehow affecting her just by holding her hand. Something was happening. Changing. The exchange was not just on her. He felt his pulse quicken and a thrill of exhilaration shoot through him. Some of that was his desire but he was also on high alert.

*What the hell is happening?*

He fought to maintain the connection. It was like riding a razors edge, threatening to overwhelm him…and maybe them both. His bear energy was so powerful, and she was letting it come into her; he sensed her giving herself over to it, letting it seep through her skin and imprint on her. Marking her heart and soul in the most wonderful way.

They turned a corner and the main park of Misty Vale spread out ahead of them. The big old iron gates had been locked, but with Smith being from one of the founding families of Misty Vale, and having organized Oktoberfest, he had the key to open them and get inside. He felt Stella's eyes on him as he pulled it from his coat pocket and began to unlock them, her gaze then flitting ahead, taking in the big tents that had been set up, and the little town of its own that had been created.

"We wanted it to reflect traditional Bavarian festivals," he said. "When we started this, we didn't really have a clue what we were doing. But with each year that's passed by, and with us taking trips to Germany ourselves, we know, now, what works, and we'd like to think that we've captured it nicely."

He watched as her eyes widened with intrigue as they stepped through the gates and moved into the main part of the festival. They had set the tents up so that they created walkways, almost like little streets of their own.

"We have our own little neighborhoods within these gates," Smith explained. "We have the gift and shopping tent neighborhood." He pointed toward some of the stalls that had been set up but all the stock was missing still and would be filled in the morning as the vendors came in. "And we have the farm produce section." He pointed to another lane of tents that ran in another direction.

"It really does feel like a little town of its own in here," Stella laughed. And Smith was glad that she could see his vision.

"Then we have the traditional German produce, which we've sourced, that's going to be going there. And we have some of the town's own stores, selling our own ales and crafts, and, of course, your aunt's stall will be over there... I think that's her tent."

He pointed into the distance, to another lane of tents. Stella smiled at this, and he could feel her warmth. She loved the fact that her aunt was involved, he could tell.

"And then we have the beer tents, which all culminate in the center and the main attraction..." They kept walking, and Stella looked around, her eyes taking it all in.

It was kind of like a maze of tents, all in rows, leading to the center of the park where the main part of the festival had been arranged. As the tents began to end, Stella clapped her hands together, and he heard her gasp.

"Oh, wow," she said. "This looks amazing!"

And she was right.

It truly did… And this was before anyone had arrived, and it was completely unlit and shadowed in darkness.

They had a tall teepee covering the very center of the park and underneath were fire pits and benches with fur blankets; but on the other side, there was a stage set up out in the open air where bands could play and a dance area for people to let loose and have fun. It was such a large space, but it had been done tastefully and allowed for the best area, smack-dab in the middle of the event, to showcase even more of Misty Vale's treats. There was another bar in the teepee, serving only Misty Vale or Bavarian Ales, and there were other beer tents flanking it outside, along with more tables and seating areas in the open air.

"I love it," she said as she looked at him, and when he caught her eye, it made his heard thump harder.

"It took us a little while to get it right," he admitted. "Like I say, our first couple of years of doing this festival didn't look anywhere near as good. But I think we're doing okay now."

"You're doing better than okay," she said.

Smith found himself moving close to her, their eyes locked in on each other's and a silence rising between them. He could see the look in her, one that said she wanted this. She wanted him. And his bear stirred even harder, it was clawing at the surface beneath his skin and he had to subdue it.

"I'm very glad I met you, Stella," Smith said honestly.

She reached out and took hold of his hand, her palm squeezing his and his heat rising even more. His entire body felt on fire, as if her touch was setting something off in him, turning him into a better man. She took a step closer, and above them, the stars twinkled brightly in the night sky. He felt the gravity of the situation. To be there with her, a girl with dragon magic and family with dragon blood... But he couldn't stop this, and neither could she. What was happening between them was too consuming and powerful.

He reached up and stroked the side of her face; she closed her eyes and bit her lip as if his touch had done something to her, making her physically ache, but in the right way.

His heart pounded, and he could hear the thump of his pulse in his ears. His hot bear blood was coursing through him, radiating out of his palms and as he touched her, he could tell that she was feeling it too, and it was calming her. She leaned into him and then she slowly opened her eyes.

She reached up and wrapped her arms around his neck, staring deeply into his eyes. Smith reached around her waist and put his hands on her hips. She felt so tiny in his arms, but as he leaned in to kiss her, he knew her soul matched his, and that this was meant to be.

When their lips met, it was as if fireworks had been let off all around them. He had heard some of his kind talk about what it meant to find a mate, but this was like nothing he could ever have imagined. It was as if his brain was on high alert, as if every sensation felt deeper, more intense and harder.

She moaned as she pressed herself against him, her ample chest pushing against his torso and her arms pulling him in tightly. She was opening herself to him, wanting him, and with each kiss and slip of their tongues, Smith knew that he wasn't going to be able to walk away from this girl. No matter how hard he may have initially tried.

When their lips broke apart and she smiled up at him, he saw a glint in her eye. It was his bear, being echoed back to him. He had possessed part of her, and she knew it.

"Does this not scare you?" he whispered, holding her still and feeling the heat power between them.

"No, not at all." She smiled and then bit her lip. "I know what you are, Smith… And I know what I just felt. It was extraordinary."

Hearing her say the words and knowing she was happy for this and without reservation, made his heart sing.

"It was extraordinary," he said. "But I am a bear, Stella…" he said, without wanting to ruin the moment. "What about your family? What will they feel about this?"

Stella shook her head slowly, her eyes not leaving his.

"This is why I always hated this town," she said sadly. "For some reason, everyone has to be so involved in everyone else's business."

"The shifter packs here have to stay civil," he said. "Can you imagine how quickly things could get out of hand if they didn't?"

"I guess," she said. "But I'm not a shifter. I'm not even part dragon… I just have family members who are, and I've been touched by their magic. I know I easily could have been, but I'm not. I'm all human… And I know how I feel."

Smith smiled and he leaned in and kissed her again.

"You do realize what it means to be with a shifter bear," he said mischievously. "It means things between us are going to get pretty serious, pretty fast."

"Oh, I know all the legends…" she said. "The way shifters work. I've heard about my own family and what happens when they find someone…" She looked at him wistfully.

*How did I get so lucky?*

How had he met a girl who was so fucking cool with all of this? At some level though he knew it was more than luck. The girls he had dated in the past had all been so terrified of him when they had learned he was a little bit different. But not Stella; she was one of a kind too. She knew her own mind and she wasn't afraid to explore the unknown.

It was all so right.

"I mean, I may need a little more information, of course," she half-laughed. "But I want to know it all. I want to know you."

"I want to know you too," he said, squeezing her hips tightly as he wrapped his arms around her and pulled her even closer to him.

He was so hard and turned on, but he had to wait. He could see the look in her eyes too, as if she wanted to rip his clothes off and ravish him, but she was holding back. She had self-control, just as much as he had.

Smith was about to kiss her again, when, suddenly, their quiet little escape in the center of the park and Oktoberfest was shattered. The gate to the park slammed and he heard the roar of laughter coming with it. Stella jumped back and away from him, as if she were afraid that they were doing something wrong, and then they both looked at each other and smirked. It made it even more exciting.

Smith knew who was coming their way; it was his bear brothers.

"It's my pack," he whispered lowly.

Stella winked, and they stepped even further apart, both of them wanting to keep their secret just that for a little while longer. It was unsaid between them, but he knew she felt the same way.

"Smith?" Archer's voice cut through the night and stillness of the park.

"I'm here," he called back. "By the center teepee."

He winked at Stella, and she had to try and hide her wide grin. He could tell she was trying not to laugh, and when the pack of bears began to appear from around the sides of the other tents, he saw the way they were all looking at him. It was with suspicion and intrigue.

"Well, well, well," Brandon said with a wry smile. "And what do we have here?"

The bears were drunk, he could sense it in them, and he wasn't far off himself. There had been a lot of booze flowing at Archer's bar, and they had a lot to celebrate, but that didn't mean Smith wanted them to start getting too leery, and he put his hands on his hips to show his size.

Bear politics at their finest. The alphas were always sizing each other up.

"I'm just showing Stella here around our wonderful festival," he said, non plussed. "She's back in town and new to all of this, and she's going to be helping her aunt out on one of the stores. You know Camille with the candies?" he asked.

The bears all looked at each other and smirked. He knew the drill; he had been on the other side with them plenty of times, but that didn't make him any less on his guard. He knew they were going to give him a tough time over this.

"Oh, Camille? With Treasured Sweets on Main Street?" Archer asked. "Isn't she part of the dragon family?"

They were full of mischief and all the bears began to jeer and nudge each other, casting their glances at Stella, who was staring them down. She didn't look fazed by them, rather like she was bored instead, and she cast her glance at Smith and rolled her eyes. It made him smirk.

"I was just saying to Smith, how I remember why I left this town," she said sassily. "Too many outdated attitudes."

"Oooh," Brandon laughed. "She's feisty!"

Smith held up his hand to call time on the teasing. He wasn't about to let this get out of hand and for them to start being too much.

"Okay, guys," he said sternly. "You've made your point and had your fun."

Archer looked at him for a moment, and it was clear that, for a split second, it could have gone either way. They may have been brothers and pack members – they may have killed for each other and been sworn together by oath and blood – but that didn't mean they wouldn't get into it if they pushed each other hard enough. There had been plenty of times, over the years, when they had all fought and warred with each other, blood had been shed between them, but they had always remained a strong and loyal pack. They kept their eyes fixed on each other, and it was clear that the rest of the pack, and even Stella, could feel the tension.

She took a step back, and Archer's eyes flickered to her.

"Threatening your pack for a dragon girl," Archer said with a raised brow. "This is an interesting development."

"She isn't a dragon," Smith said.

"Close enough," Archer said.

The tension in the air could have been cut with a knife, with Smith standing his ground and looking on sternly, his lip almost curled. He didn't know how it had gotten so out of hand, so fast, but he was relieved when Archer's shoulders sagged and he laughed.

"Well, fuck!" Archer said. "These festivals always bring out the best and worst in us, don't they?" He started to laugh, and the mood relaxed.

"I'll say," Smith breathed out deeply, feeling himself untighten.

"Welcome back to Misty Vale, Stella," Archer said, and some of the other pack members echoed his words. "As you seem to remember, us bears can be a handful... I'm sure your cousins have said similar."

Smith looked to Stella, and she just shrugged.

"I haven't seen any of them since I've been back," she said. "And it's not like we've kept in touch..."

She looked at Smith and smiled weakly.

"Well," Archer said. "It's good to have you here, and I look forward to working with you at the festival."

"Likewise," Stella said, but Smith could hear the hint of annoyance on the edge of her voice. And he couldn't blame her; the bears were notoriously hard work when it came to the feud between them and the dragons.

"Come on," Smith said, "I'll show you out. And you lot, wait here, will you?" He looked at the bear pack, and they all smiled.

Smith felt enraged still, as if they had come looking for trouble. But he knew they had been drinking and hadn't seen anything with him and Stella, but that didn't mean they couldn't tell. Hell, it must have been plain as day. He tried not to bristle too much or think about the fact that they had been driving him so mad lately that he had nearly left town over it. It was time to forget it and move on.

Stella and Smith walked out of the teepee and toward the tents, moving between them, and going toward the gates.

"They are intense." She looked at him and half-laughed. "Plus, are they always so charming and friendly?"

"I'm sorry," Smith said, cringing. "They've had a lot to drink, and you know the history. But I can't say that's an excuse. I'll be talking to them about it."

He reached for Stella's hand covertly, in case anyone was still watching them, and then they picked up their pace as they went to the gate.

"I'm going to have to go back," he said as he looked into her eyes. "But let me get you in a cab?"

She nodded and smiled at him before they kissed again.

"I don't know how I'll ever thank you," she said. "First, saving me on the mountain; then, towing my car... Then, this, protecting me from some wild bear shifters."

"Oh, I can surely think of something," he said mischievously. "You can let me take you out properly."

He stared deeply into her eyes and was sure he saw himself already reflecting back in her gaze. His bear was getting underneath her skin, and she was welcoming him in.

"Okay," she said. "I'd like that."

Smith smiled again, and she pushed herself up on her tiptoes to plant a solitary kiss on his lips before she began to move away. Smith raised his arm into the air and whistled, and a taxi that had been waiting on the other side of the street started up and pulled around to park next to Stella.

He watched as she opened the door and looked back at him.

"I'll call you tomorrow," he said.

"I'll be at the store all day," she said with a wry smile. "Why don't you come and find me instead…"

He liked it. It sounded like a challenge and a game.

"Okay, then," he smiled. "I'll find you, Stella…"

She ducked down into the back seat of the cab and slammed the door, and he stood there watching as it pulled away.

He'd had one of the best nights in a long while, and he knew he had found something incredible in Stella. Now, he just had to throw his pack off the scent of their blossoming union… And somehow, get through Oktoberfest without killing any of them.

*It's going to be an interesting week.*

## CHAPTER 9

Stella woke the next morning with the taste of Smith on her lips, and her entire body writhing with lust. It had been such a whirlwind since she had come back to Misty Vale, but now, she had given in to her urges and her heart's desire… And she and Smith had taken things further.

She stretched and smiled, looking over to the clock on the wall and seeing that it was almost 8am. She had climbed quietly out of the cab the previous evening, snuck into the back of the house, grabbed a bottle of water from the refrigerator and made her way upstairs as quietly as possible. She hadn't heard Camille yet, but she wondered if she had been listening and waiting for her to come home. She could imagine that leaving her back in Archer's had been torture for her, especially considering the fact that the bears had all been in there, drinking and chatting loudly, playing pool and generally making themselves known. But Stella also knew that Camille wasn't stupid, and she wasn't going to try to prevent her from seeing Smith if she truly wanted to. Maybe she just didn't want to hear about it… And then, if her cousins came knocking or had a bad reaction to it all, she could say she didn't know a whole lot. Stella didn't want to put Camille in an awkward position either, so she decided this was the best way to move forward... Not hiding anything important, but rather being selective with the information. She was an adult, after all, and didn't need to feel as if she had to get permission.

"Funny how you can slip back into old habits," Stella whispered to herself. Thinking of how she had always gone to Camille for guidance when she had been a kid and a teen growing up in this very house. Was it any wonder she felt the need to seek her aunt's approval?

She pushed herself up and blinked her bleary eyes. She wasn't hungover but she could feel that she had drank the night before and she quickly took the water from the nightstand and finished it off. When she jumped into the shower, she felt as if she were being revived and washing away the excess from the previous evening, and by the time she was downstairs, getting herself a coffee from the coffee maker, she was basically back to normal.

"Ahh, so you did come home...." Camille said cheerily as she stepped in from the hallway and came blustering into the kitchen. "For a moment, there, this morning, I wasn't sure."

"You didn't wait up for me then?" Stella half laughed.

"Wait up? Are you kidding me? I've got a million and one things to do today, and I'm already running late." She reached out and grabbed a pastry from a covered basket on the counter and then dashed toward the back door. "I've left the keys to the store right here." She tapped the counter, and Stella saw them. "And I'll just be on the other end of the phone if you need me. Open the store at ten, please, dear!"

"Okay," Stella called back to her, but Camille was already out the door, and it was slamming closed behind her, carried by the wind.

She heard Camille's car start, and it made her think of her own... And then, by default, Smith, yet again. Man, he was so hot. Kissing him and holding his hand, had been an experience. She had been able to feel the animal power deep within him, and she felt changed when their lips met.

She smiled and touched her neck, still feeling his heat there, lurking beneath her skin. How was she going to deal with not seeing him again right away? She knew he had said he would come find her today... But that could be hours from now... And she wanted to see him right this second. She wanted to be close to him, to feel his rock-hard abs and body pressed up against her, to feel his lips on hers and trailing down her neck.

She had to stop daydreaming as she started to become too hot and turned on. And she shook her head to snap herself out of it.

Instead, she glanced up to the clock. It was half past eight and she still had to dry her hair, do her make-up, pick a cute outfit and get the hell down to Treasured Sweets by, no later than, nine thirty to make sure she could open on time.

"Nothing like a hectic start to the day," she mused.

And it was sure to only get even crazier. It was the beginning of Oktoberfest... And as she was beginning to learn, anything could happen.

BY THE TIME IT HIT THE AFTERNOON LULL, STELLA HAD SERVED what could easily have been over a hundred customers. They had taken thousands of dollars' worth of sales, and the whole of Misty Vale was so full of excitement that it felt as if there had been an explosion of festive Bavarian cheer throughout every street and building.

She leaned back against the counter and sighed. She

hadn't stopped for hours; her back was beginning to ache, and her feet were killing her, but she felt so happy that she didn't mind. This store and working in it was so much fun, and she loved it already. Back in the city, her roles had all been so boring and dull. Working in offices or in stiff retail environments, she had constantly felt like she was being watched and judged. Here, she called the shots, and she loved the atmosphere; it was so magical.

She couldn't believe it when she checked the time and it was almost five. A whole day had flown by, and with the doors to Main Street flung open, she could hear the music drifting up from the festival and filtering out of the bars nearby. There was a crisp autumn chill in the air, and it was already beginning to get dark. She thought about closing up and heading down to the festival to see what it was all about, but now that it was starting to slow in the shop, and she had real time to think, she felt a little nag of disappointment that she hadn't yet seen Smith. He had said he was going to find her, after all.

Then, suddenly, as if he had read her mind, and they were already connected by some deep invisible force, she had the feeling inside of her that he was near. She felt her body respond to him, she felt her lips tingle, and she reached up and touched them, smiling and feeling their heat. She could feel the sensation of his hands on her hips, as if his touch had left a memory on her and was drawing her back into it as he grew closer.

When she looked up to the doorway, Smith was walking inside, his eyes bright and his smile wide, and looking so goddam hot and sexy that she didn't know how she wasn't going to jump his bones right there and then. She felt her skin begin to heat up and her heart race.

*Fuck, he's too good to be true.*

"Hey there, shop girl," he said with a wink as he closed the door quietly behind him and turned the sign so that it read, 'Closed'.

Stella laughed and cocked her head to the side; he looked back at her with mischief.

"Can I help you, sir?" she asked in jest, putting her best customer service face forward.

"I think so…" he said, his voice trailing off as he began to look around the room, both of them easily slipping into the role playing. "I've been told there's something rare and sweet here, and I'd like to find it."

Stella raised her eyebrows and stepped out from behind the counter.

"Is that so?" she asked. "I'm not sure I have anything that matches that description for sale…"

Smith smirked and bit his bottom lip now, his eyes twinkling and his pupils wide. She could see the animal nature in him, the bear lurking beneath the surface and the power he was trying to subdue. She wanted him so badly, and yet, there was so much tension between them that it was making the air pulse. He took another step closer, and she hung back coyly, staring at him with wide, innocent eyes.

"It's definitely not for sale," he said. "But I feel like I'm getting closer…" He stopped in front of her and looked down at her. Being so close to him again was almost too much to handle. The night before had been so perfect, and him coming into the store and acting all alpha and masculine, clearly wanting to take what was his, was sending her into a frenzy.

"You can take it," she whispered, her heart almost catching in her throat. "I think I'd like you to have it."

He reached up and stoked her face and she felt the heat in his fingertips. It sent a wave of longing all over her, her skin pounding and yearning for him even more.

"When can you get off?" he said, his fingers resting on her throat so gently but sexily that it made her gasp.

"Now," she said, not even thinking about it.

"Are you sure?" he laughed, likely knowing that she shouldn't just be shutting up shop and bailing on such an important day... But he had turned her on so much, and now, she was yearning for him. She didn't want to wait a moment longer.

"My aunt will kill me," she whispered breathlessly. "But I think it would be worth it."

Smith laughed, leaned in and kissed her softly on the lips.

"What we don't want is to give her any more reason to hate me," he said with a cheeky smile. "Why don't you feel her out and see what she says? You don't have to tell her I'm here..."

Stella knew he was being sensible, and she should thank him for it, but my God, she wanted him so badly.

"I know you're right," she said with a slight huff and pout. "Hang on... Give me a minute."

She moved out of his hold, even though she didn't want to, and she picked up the phone on the counter. Smith smiled at her mischievously as she dialed Camille's number, and then he cast a quick glance back to make sure there wasn't anyone who was approaching the store, looking like they may want to be inside.

Camille answered on the third ring, and Stella could instantly hear the frivolities in the background. It sounded as if it was all going off with a bang down at the festival, and it made her feel as if she were both missing out on that and also quality time with Smith. But she also had to acknowledge her new responsibilities.

"Hi Aunt Camille," she said. "How's it been going this afternoon? It certainly sounds as if things are kicking off well down there!"

"Oh, it's been wonderful, dear!" Camille shouted down the line, clearly unable to hear very well at her end due to the band playing loudly in the background and all the voices and chatter. "I've even tried my first traditional ale, and I have to say, I quite liked it! You'll have to come down and run the stall too. We can switch it up so that you don't miss out."

"That would be great!" Stella called to her. "I was just wondering what time you would normally close up? It's after five and things have been slowing here over the past couple of hours… And now, it seems like the majority of footfall on Main Street may have moved to the restaurants and B&B's before people go down to the festival."

"Yes, I can imagine it's getting pretty quiet up there," Camille agreed. "If you want to wrap things up now, you can. My stall will be closing here in the next half an hour, and then I'll be heading back up to the shop to open for the last hour or so later, once people have finished dinner. Sometimes, we get a rush between eight and nine thirty."

"Okay," Stella said. "As long as you're sure? I have a few things I need to do…"

"It's no problem, sweetheart," Camille said. "I appreciate you doing such a good job today. I can't believe how much we've sold!"

"It's been a good day, that's for sure. However, maybe it's beginner's luck…"

"I very much doubt it…"

In the background on Camille's end, Stella could hear the noise level rising, and it sounded as if some customers had come over to her stall.

"I'm going to have to go, dear," Camille said. "But lock up and put a note on the door saying we'll be open again at 8pm."

"Okay, Aunt Camille, I will," Stella said before she ended

the call and looked back to Smith, who was standing nonchalantly against the counter, watching her with a wide grin.

"Well," she said. "I think we're good to go…"

Smith punched the air in mock winner's glory, and Stella laughed. She loved how playful and fun he was with things like this; it made her like him even more.

She quickly closed down the computer, made sure the back door was locked and the appropriate lights were left on, and then she wrote out the note and grabbed her purse.

"So… I guess, the big question is, where are you taking me?" she asked with a raised brow.

Smith slipped his hand into hers as they headed toward the door, the note firmly in her grip.

"You'll have to wait and see." He smiled as they headed out onto Main Street.

# CHAPTER 10

As they walked away from Treasured Sweets and down Main Street, Smith was totally caught up in this bubble of romance with Stella. From the moment they had met, he had felt great things, but now, they had kissed, she knew what he was, and things were moving quickly. The previous evening had been stressful with the pack, but it had been manageable. Now, they were wandering in plain sight of anyone in Misty Vale, and he wondered if her cousins had caught word of what may potentially be going on with them.

His truck was parked on the other side of the street, and the footfall and traffic were ramping up as plenty of people began to head down to Oktoberfest. He could see Stella looking longingly in that direction, as if she wanted, so desperately, to be there, and he didn't want to pull her away into obscurity. They had to be strong about this and not care too much about what their respective families may think.

He paused for a moment, and he could feel Stella's eyes on him, waiting for answers.

"How about we go down to the festival?" he said. "I don't want you to miss out on it. Plus, you've got to see how much fun they're all having. We can drink ale, eat Bratwursts, maybe even get some lederhosen and join one of the dancing competitions."

Stella's eyes brightened and she laughed.

"That sounds perfect," she said. "However, I think we can skip the lederhosen."

Smith laughed too, and they began to walk hand in hand, their palms so hot and sealed together, and their union becoming stronger and more unbreakable by the second.

When they reached the main gates of the park, the crowds were surging and so many people were there. It made it feel like such a success that Smith had to feel proud, even if it was just for a moment. He and his pack had come together, with some of the people of the town, and created a great event for so many people. Now that it was alive and living all on its own, it made it even more rewarding. He knew, now, that they had cracked it when it came to hosting large-scale events and it made him excited for the future; especially, now that they had the added clout of some biker gang on board. It was sure to drive the dragons wild.

They wandered through the crowds and toward the main teepee. It was so busy there that Smith knew that even if they did see anyone who could potentially have a problem with them, they likely wouldn't even notice. There wouldn't be a real chance for them to speak.

They stopped at one of the beer tents, and Smith bought them each a big tankard of Bavarian ale, and then they walked closer to the main action. Bands were playing, and people were dancing, the fire pits were already lit, and the atmosphere was magical. He looked down at Stella and could feel her happiness. It didn't seem like they had only known each other for a matter of days; their souls were so well connected that it was as if there had been something between them before, as if, surely, they had always been together on some level ,and it made him feel so at home with her.

They stopped and watched the bands playing and some groups dancing in front of the stage. Smith let his shoulder lean into Stella and his arm creep around her back so that he could hold her under her coat. Her skin was hot, and she leaned into him more closely, looking up at him with wide eyes and smiling coyly. He knew what was on her mind, and he knew what was on his… But they were right in the middle of Oktoberfest, surrounded by so many people. She bit her lip and grinned and then she sipped her ale, letting her free hand creep around his back too and squeezing him slightly as if she were trying to encourage him. He had been so good and had resisted so much, but now, when they were so into each other, were so hot for one another, and were caught up in this party atmosphere, he knew he didn't want to keep denying her or them.

"Just feeling your hand on my bare skin is turning me on," he said to her, and she looked up at him with lust in her eyes.

"Then let's do something about it," she said knowingly.

He moved backward, and they began to walk away from the teepee and out the back of the festival, behind all the power and service vans, and out toward the back gate of the park that led to a vast patch of woodland. Smith had a key for the back gate with him, being one of the organizers, and he reached into his pocket and pulled it free, before he slipped it into the lock and opened the iron gate, letting them slip through and locking it again behind them.

He grabbed Stella's hand and began to run with her, and she squealed a little with excitement. They quickly disappeared into the forest, leaving the festival behind, but taking the sounds of fun and music with them, carried through the trees as if by magic. It was so dark in the forest, that as they went farther, he had to use his bear senses to ensure they were safe. He could sense no one was close by, and that they were truly alone, so when Stella finally grabbed him and pulled him to a stop, and he took hold of her by the waist and pushed her gently up against a tree, he knew he didn't have to worry about them being caught.

Their lips met in a frenzy and as his tongue parted her lips and flicked up against hers, he felt himself take her breath away. She gasped and melted into him, her arms wrapping around his neck and her moans of pleasure growing stronger. They had been so good to deny themselves when they had such an instant and passionate connection, but now, here in the deep woodland of Misty Vale, there was no turning back. Their bodies needed each other, and they were so hot and turned on; they knew what they both wanted.

Smith was so hard, and his cock was engorged; his bear was rumbling away beneath the surface of his skin, desperate to claim her and make her his. He knew how much she wanted him, and she reached down for his belt buckle, unsnapping it quickly and slipping her hand down and into his underwear, her fingers wrapping around his length and making him groan. She gasped too, feeling how hard he was for her, at his impressive girth and length. She moved her hand, jacking him slowly, sending a wave of heat and pleasure rocketing through his entire being. God, she was good, and with each stroke of her hand, it sent him further into a passionate fluster. He let his hand squeeze her breasts, and she moaned and smiled against his lips. Smith reached for her pants, quickly undid the buttons and slipped his hand inside, searching for her sacred place and feeling her breathing becoming much more frantic and shorter. When he moved her panties to one side and parted her legs, he found her pussy- hot and wet and wanting him- and it almost sent him over the edge. He rubbed her clit, and she almost buckled, her knees giving way slightly as he worked her over. Her whole frame was juddering, and she whimpered and gasped, as he slid a finger inside of her and she threw back her head, opening her legs wider to let him get in deeper as she tried to keep up the pace on his cock.

Above them, the stars were piercing through the trees, and the music from the festival was drifting through to meet them. Smith's bear senses were heightened, and he growled deeply, unable to hold it in any longer as Stella squeezed his finger with her pussy walls and came in a crashing wave of passion. She gasped and fell against him, and he held her there with his free hand, supporting her as her body bucked against his and her juices slicked his hand. Feeling her in this way, with her pleasure covering his hand, made him unravel too, and he came hot and hard in her hand seconds later. They both writhed against the tree, adoring each other and unable to deny themselves any longer.

Stella leaned back against the tree and gasped, her chest heaving and glistening with sweat, as Smith kissed her and grunted, his bear satisfied but also eager for more. She smiled and looked deeply into his eyes, and he knew he had found his one. *His "person". His mate.* She was everything. He wanted to claim her so badly, to fuck her and make her come again and again, but they had to make sure they were ready and that she knew what it would mean for them for the rest of time.

"You're a bad man, Smith Savage," Stella said mischievously as he pushed his weight on her and kissed her again. "And I wouldn't have it any other way."

Smith smiled down at her, and he knew he felt exactly the same way. In each other, they had found something special… And now, there was no turning back.

# CHAPTER 11

When they walked out of the forest together, Stella felt like a naughty school kid, but it was oh, so worth it. They had snuck out of the Oktoberfest and into the woods, away from the prying eyes of the town, and they had given in to their urges. It had felt raw and real, in that moment, as if it was meant to be. She looked up at Smith and smirked, and he looked down at her adoringly. She had never felt this way about someone before, and to be there with him, as they walked back into the crowds of people, made it feel even more special that they had their little secret. He wrapped his arm around her shoulder, and they disappeared into the mass of tents, stopping to buy wine and beer and then making their way back to the main teepee to sit and watch the music and entertainment by the firepits.

They found a good table, and Stella pulled the blankets over her knees.

"It's a real nice touch the way you do this," she said. "Putting blankets out for people if they want them."

"Sure, if it means they're comfortable," he smiled. "Then they'll stay longer and buy more beer and food."

He winked, and Stella laughed.

"The ultimate businessman," she teased.

"Hey, we are," he said genuinely. "There's a lot you don't yet know about the way of business in Misty Vale and my part in it."

Stella smiled. She couldn't wait to hear about it all: about his life, his upbringing, the way he had thrived in this town when she had done nothing but want to escape. It was strange that they had such different experiences when it came to their lives there, but somehow, they found each other, at this moment in time, and they had forged this bond. She had never really believed in fate before… But her coming back to Misty Vale after such a long time, and him being out there on the road in that exact moment when she needed help… It was as if the stars had aligned for them.

She took a sip of her wine and then looked out over the crowd. A group had formed on the edge of where people were dancing, and there was something about them that looked familiar. She paused for a moment, and then her heart sank a little. She couldn't be one hundred percent sure from a distance, but it looked an awful lot like her cousins.

She turned her head slightly to hide her main profile, and she looked at Smith with a sheepish smile.

"What's the matter?" he asked her.

Stella paused for a moment, wondering if he would see them; his eyes went over the top of her head and she saw them rest on the direction of the group. From his reaction and the way his expression clouded over momentarily, she knew he had clocked them.

"Your cousins," he said with a slight bristle. "It looks like they're over there…"

Stella winced and nodded.

"I haven't spoken to or seen them in years," she tried to reassure him.

"It doesn't matter," he said warmly to her, squeezing her hand. "This is Misty Vale… and it won't be forgotten, because you have not been forgotten. You're their family."

She clenched her teeth and nodded.

She had wondered if this would happen, if she would run into her cousins and if they would cause trouble for her, or whether they would simply pass her by. But she felt something deep in her gut, as if she had picked up some of Smith's intuition. She just knew and had the feeling that things were about to go bad… Just like they almost had the night before with the bears.

She braced herself and then she turned, looking at the group and seeing, who she believed to be Striker, staring back at her through the crowd with dark eyes.

Striker Livingstone, the cousin she hadn't seen since she was sixteen. He was looking at her with so much disdain that she almost felt floored. This was not going to be good.

She turned away and tried to rise to her feet, but Smith gently pushed her knee down before she could.

"Don't worry," he said, smiling at her reassuringly. "I'll handle them if they come over."

She smiled and tried to remain calm. She loved the fact that Smith was so strong and protective, and she knew he would do everything to make sure they didn't hassle her… But she was still dreading being the cause of an argument that was clearly only going to ignite a fire that had long been smoldering between the bear and dragon packs for generations. Stella could easily be the log thrown on that was going to bring it roaring back to life.

She didn't know how she knew, but she could sense that they were coming over, and she closed her eyes and took a breath.

She had to rationalize with herself that it was going to happen at some point, and she was going to have to face it head on. Now, she had a rush of understanding why her aunt had shown concern. She hadn't wanted Stella to go through something like this and to feel unwanted or like an outcast by her family in Misty Vale... But it appeared that love was going to come at a price.

"Stella?" the voice cut through the tension from behind her, and she turned slowly to see her cousins standing there.

Striker. Dash. Zane.

Three powerful dragon shifters who had been such a big part of her childhood. She may not have seen them in ten years but there was no denying that it was them. And it was clear that they knew it was her too. She smiled and rose to her feet, and they all embraced her one by one, hugging her tightly, and she felt the magic in them all over again after so long, the dragons inside of them so powerful and prominent.

When she stepped back, and they were all in a circle, Smith rose to his feet too, and he put his hand on Stella's shoulder. He saw her cousins' eyes go to it immediately, and Striker smiled curtly, his eyes narrowing.

"I can't believe you finally came home, Stella," he said, looking only at her and not acknowledging Smith. "I had heard it, but I didn't know whether to believe it was true."

"Yes," she smiled. "A few days ago, now. I didn't think I would ever say it, but it's good to be back."

Striker and the dragons all looked at each other and smiled.

"And you're back staying with Aunt Camille?" Zane asked.

Stella nodded.

"It's so good to be with her again," Stella said. "I've missed her. I mean, we have never gone a long time without seeing one another, and she had visited me plenty of times in the city, but it's different being back here. It feels more natural."

"How many years has it been?" Striker asked. "Since you last set foot in this town?"

"Ten years," she half-laughed.

Striker smiled and nodded.

"Well, it looks as if you've found plenty of reasons to be here…" Striker said eventually, his eyes flickering over at Smith. "And you've also certainly been very busy."

Stella felt herself tense.

*Here we go…* she thought.

Smith's grip on her shoulder tightened slightly, and she reached up and rested her hand on top of his before she looked into his eyes and smiled.

"You have bear energy all over you," Striker said waspishly. "Not the best look for someone in a dragon family."

Stella gave pause, and she looked from one cousin to the next, searching their eyes for something that may give them away, something that may lead her to think they were joking. But they all looked rather serious and not in the mood for jokes.

"I'm not a dragon, Striker…" she said warily. "I'm human."

His eyes narrowed again, and he looked annoyed.

"We all know that's not the point, cousin," he said with venom.

She had never seen this side of them before, and it wasn't something she was enjoying. The cousins she knew had always looked out for her, and now, she was being targeted as if she had broken some unholy law. She looked down and shook her head. She felt fixed to the spot, unable even to blink. Her heart was racing away beneath her skin. She could feel her cousins' anger, but she could also feel something else more strongly… Smith's protective energy and the fact that he wasn't about to let this slide.

"I think you boys need to calm down," he said as he stepped in front of Stella and held up his hands. He wasn't being confrontational, but he wasn't about to let them speak to her like that either.

"And I think you need to step back, bear..." Zane said menacingly.

The tension between them was rising at an exponential rate, and Stella didn't know how to defuse it. She didn't want them to get into a big fight, and she didn't want to alienate her cousins either. It was a tricky balance, and she looked up at Striker with pleading eyes, her soul begging him to stop it.

Smith's face cracked into an amused smile. He shook his head and laughed.

"What's so funny?" Striker asked, his eyes burning with dragon fire.

Stella had forgotten how frightening her dragon shifter cousins could be. She had been touched by their magic and so she could see the beast within them more so than regular humans. She could see the fire burning away and the way it flared up with their rage. Striker was pissed, and the tension was getting higher with each passing moment.

"Funny, I don't remember you being so relaxed when the shoe was on the other foot..." Striker said, his voice unwavering.

And the dragons all looked to one another, as if they were trying to gauge if they were on the same page, but then they burst into laughter.

"Don't be ridiculous," Smith said, shaking his head.

"Ahh yes, now, it makes sense," Zane said venomously as if the penny had just dropped. "I would advise you to be careful with him, Stella... Seems like Smith's still bitter about something that happened plenty of years ago. And these bears talk about trying to call a truce... It's pathetic."

Smith went to say something, but they were already turning away to leave. Stella reached out and pulled him back, but she felt stunned.

*What do they mean by that?*

She looked at Smith who didn't look too fazed; he shook his head and relaxed his fists. And then he looked at her and smiled weakly. He had stood his ground, and she was proud of him, but now she wanted to know what the hell they had been talking about.

"What did they just say?" she asked, carefully.

"What?" he said, his eyes still fixed firmly on her dragon cousins as they walked away, his hatred of them clear and present all over his face.

"They said something about me being careful with you… And that you were bitter about something?"

Smith looked down at her and shook his head, as if he didn't know what she was asking about.

"I think your cousins would say anything to cause trouble between us, Stella," he said. "Please, don't let them get into your head."

He slipped his hand into hers and squeezed it tightly with reassurance. But now, she had a nagging doubt building deep in her mind. She didn't know why, but what her cousins had said was reverberating through her, as if, on some level, she knew something was being left unsaid between her and Smith, and it made her nervous.

She looked back to the band playing, and she saw Striker on the other side of the dance area, his eyes reflecting the fire from the pits and pulling her back somewhere… Somewhere into her roots in this town. She had truly forgotten what it felt like to be here, and for the feuds to be prominent in so many people's lives.

She just hoped, now, for her and Smith's sake, that this ancient war wasn't about to turn into something nasty for them and ruin what they had.

# CHAPTER 12

"Okay," Stella said as she sat down at the table the next morning and huffed. Camille was sitting opposite her with wide eyes, as if she was expecting some kind of grand speech, and Stella was about to lay out some new law. It hadn't even hit 8am and it was clear to Camille that Stella was worked up.

"My cousins are assholes," Stella said. "I ran into them last night, and they said all of this stuff to Smith and me, and it's made me feel like total crap."

Camille winced and placed her cup of coffee down on the table gently.

"I tried to tell you," she said. "I didn't want you to become a target of theirs. They're fiercely protective over our family. Surely, you remember that..."

Stella tried, but all she could remember from her upbringing in Misty Vale was that she had been desperate to get the hell out of there. Now, maybe she was beginning to truly realize why. Maybe it wasn't just to be close again with the memory of her parents back in the city; maybe it was to escape all of this bullshit. The war between shifter clans and the magic that seemed to ooze from every corner of this mystical town.

"I don't recall it being as bad as this," she said. "But I sure as hell am going to address it."

"I would leave it," Camille said. "Those dragon boys are a law unto themselves, and they're not used to anyone standing up to them."

"Oh, what, because of their money and power?" Stella wanted to smirk as she said it. Her cousins did have a lot of money and power in their town, but that didn't mean they had to treat her so badly.

Camille rose to her feet and rested her hand on Stella's shoulder. When Stella looked at her, she could see her aunt's sympathy, but it was there with an edge of *I told you so...*

When she left to head out to the Oktoberfest, Stella jumped to her feet and decided to spring into action too. She had an hour and a half before she had to be at Treasured Sweets, and she wasn't about to let the morning go to waste. She was going to find her cousins, and she was going to get to the bottom of what they had said at the end of the argument the previous evening.

Even if it killed her.

* * *

Livingstone Headquarters, their main office and place of business, was on Main Street. A boutique building that dripped money and success and seemed completely out of place in this quaint little town. As Stella approached, she felt her nerves rising, but she knew she had to be brave. She had to find out the answers as to what they had been talking about the night before, and why she had felt so uneasy ever since. She had asked Smith what her cousins had meant, and he hadn't given her an answer... Ever since then, she had been churning it over, worrying and stressing on what this could mean for them, and if he was hiding something from her.

Since she had lost her parents, she had barely trusted anyone. Smith had seemed so different; she could and would have told him anything, so for him to brush her questions off as if they didn't matter had cut her deep. Now, she knew she had to find out what had gone on, and what her cousins had been saying. She had to learn the truth about this ongoing feud and why she was being pulled into the center of it.

When she pushed open the office door and stepped inside, she was shocked at the plushness of the place. It was all marble desktops, flatscreen TVs, thick and well-watered plants, and classical music playing lowly over the speakers. She faltered by the door and then she saw Dash at the back in one of the conference rooms, and he held up his hand to wave before he came walking forward.

"Stella?" he asked, a look of uncertainty on his face, his eyes flitting behind her as if to check that she was alone.

"Hi," she said, crossing her arms over her chest. She was feeling as if she was going to have to stand her ground after the previous evening, and she was going to make sure she looked the part too.

"Do you want to come into one of the conference rooms?" he asked, cocking his head to the side.

"No," she said. "I think we can talk out here."

Dash nodded, and they stepped closer toward the seating area near the main doors, and Stella found herself sighing. She hated things like this, but it had to be done.

"I didn't like last night, Dash," she said, her eyes fixing on his. "I haven't seen you guys in a decade, and suddenly, you're all surrounding me in the middle of a festival and acting that way? It doesn't seem right."

Dash breathed out deeply, as if she were testing his patience.

"And I want to know what the hell you were talking about when you mentioned Smith and the past... What was all that supposed to mean?"

Dash smirked slightly and then he shook his head.

"What, you mean, he hasn't told you about his ex-girlfriend?" He didn't say it nastily, but there was a definite hint of him being antagonistic, as if he already knew the answer and wanted to be the one to twist the knife.

Stella felt her stomach sink, and she stiffened up. She saw the look of realization cross over Dash's face, as if he was beginning to realize that maybe Smith and Stella weren't just a fling and that she had invested feelings in him, and he pulled back slightly.

"You're family, Stella, so, of course, we're going to be protective..." he began. "But, for that reason, I think you should probably know that, a few years ago, Smith was with a girl who left him for a member of our dragon clan."

The words were blunt and to the point, and at first, they just seemed to rest there, as if they were nothing and meant nothing. She found herself shrugging, as if to say, *and so what?*

"This town is tiny," she said with a shake of her head. "Do you really think it matters if he happened to date someone who ended up with one of you guys too..."

"I mean, I guess not," Dash said. "But it's also a pretty good reason to..." He petered off and looked at her sternly before continuing. "I don't know...maybe try to get revenge."

Stella felt so goddam mad, and she rose to her feet. She stared down at Dash and couldn't believe what she was hearing, but there was something that was troubling her, and it was the fact that Smith had been so quick to brush the whole thing off and offer her little to no explanation about what they could have been referring to.

"Please, stay out of my business," she said as she turned and went to walk away. "I was happy to be home until people started sticking their noses in it."

"Stella...I'm just looking out for you. All of us are just looking out for you..." Dash called after her, but she was already at the door, yanking it open and stepping out onto Main Street.

She couldn't believe what he had said, and what he had been implying, and now, all she wanted to do was get to work and distract herself with plenty of customers and a way to pass the day.

* * *

She unlocked the door to Treasured Sweets and closed it behind her before she breathed out and closed her eyes. She had not been expecting that. She was mad at Dash, but she could also see his side. She was his cousin, and the bad feeling between the bear and the dragon packs of Misty Vale had run deep for generations. But could Smith really be only into her because he wanted revenge for a past love that had left him for a member of the dragon pack?

Stella felt herself begin to spiral. She knew there was a reason why she didn't get involved with anyone like this. Her whole life, she had spent her time keeping people at a distance, afraid that she would love them and then she would lose them. Just like her mom and dad. But when she had met Smith, and had come back to Misty Vale, it had all fallen into place so perfectly, and she had felt things for him that she had never felt for anyone.

Now, all she could think was that she had been foolish.

She felt the tears welling up behind her eyes and she

marched to the back of the store and sat down at the register, her mind swirling and her heart pounding. She felt nervous and knocked off guard, and she was so full of doubt that she didn't know how she would ever come back from this.

*I should have known he was too good to be true.*

All she knew for sure was that, overnight, her doubts about their future had been thrown into chaos.

Smith sat at the bar in Archer's and cradled a beer. It had been another long day, and his head was pounding. The festival had been so successful that he knew he shouldn't complain, and yet, he could barely keep a coherent thought together, and he felt as if something was wrong. His bear instinct had been kicking in, and he had been on high alert all day, as if he were waiting for something bad to happen or be revealed.

His pack had been tetchy since he had been in confrontation with them in the park a few nights before. They were on speaking terms and he knew he hadn't done anything to truly wrong them, but he sensed they were not happy about him and Stella seeing each other, and it had begun to really grate on him.

He had been having enough stress with them as it was before he had added to the mix. He had never enjoyed the long-standing feud in this town; it had been something that had plagued him. He didn't understand it, and it wore him down, always feeling like he was looking over his shoulder or like there was a reason that the dragons were going to come after him, his pack and their businesses, when, really, they should have complemented each other. The bears were heavily into construction, and the dragons had a property empire. Surely, they should be coming together to make their town a better place rather than driving it further apart?

Smith knew there were always two sides to every story, but he had been irritated with the dragons when they had confronted him and Stella at the Oktoberfest. He felt like they were deliberately trying to cause trouble. But he had to admit, neither pack were innocent. Over the years, they had all done things to cause trouble for the other. It was just that he was in the firing line yet again.

He thought about what they had thrown out there and said in front of Stella; the fact that his ex-girlfriend had left him for a dragon shifter. It had been so long ago and had barely even crossed his mind when he and Stella had met, because he was too busy being blown away by her. He knew that, at the time, he had been cut up about it, and it was something that had niggled away at him over the years. He knew his ex- girlfriend had been unfaithful, and for her to throw in the added insult of running off with a dragon pack member, had only made it harder to come to terms with. It was an old wound, but one he had dealt with… And now, it looked as if it were rearing its ugly head. His own pack was putting pressure on him, and now, the dragons were circling, looking for a weakness in his defense, and he didn't like it one bit.

*And then, there's Stella.*

*What is she thinking? What if she isn't even that into me? Have I just been creating a fantasy?*

*… And what if the dragons put her up to all this?*

He stopped still, the beer bottle millimeters from his lips, and his mouth went dry. Thought coming a mile a minute, bouncing around in his head. The dragons were so cunning, and over the years, plenty of things had gone down between their packs to make them doubt their own sanity and to cause trouble for their prospective businesses. *What if, somehow, the dragons had realized I was leaving town and they had wanted to pull me back by planting Stella there to lure me? What if she has been in on it all along?* He didn't know why they would want to do this, but if they were just wanting to cause trouble or to throw a cloud over Oktoberfest, then he couldn't truly put it past the dragons. Especially now that they were probably beginning to get wind of the fact that the biker gang, The Forsaken Riders, had arrived in town and were starting to do business with the bears.

He rubbed his temples and shook his head.

This was complete madness. What was he even thinking?

What he and Stella had experienced together couldn't be faked. It was strong, raw and real. He had fallen in love with her and he felt so connected to her that it couldn't be anything else but fate. Surely.

But now... Now, he couldn't get the thought out of his head.

He slammed the bottle down on the wooden bar top and sighed.

"What's up?" Archer asked as he wandered along the bar and leaned back against the refrigerators.

"Everything just feels a bit...fucked..." he said, but then he laughed and shook his head. The last thing he was about to do was give away how he was feeling, even to his bear brother. It just wasn't the sort of thing his kind did. They were good at hiding how they were truly feeling and keeping it stored away, releasing their frustrations when they turned into bear form instead.

"We've got a lot to be grateful for at the moment, brother." Archer smiled as he raised his own bottle and held it out to chink against Smith's. Smith tipped his to meet it, and then they both took a sip.

He knew Archer was right, but he couldn't settle.

He was going to go find Stella.

* * *

BY THE TIME HE REACHED TREASURED SWEETS, IT WAS ALL closed up for the evening. He looked for a note on the door like the one Stella had left a day or so before, but there wasn't anything this time. Instead, it appeared as if the shop had been fully closed up for the night.

"Weird," he said, as he looked back in the direction of the festival and listened to the way the noise of the chatter and music was drifting over.

*Why would Camille not want to open again that night? Surely, it was going to be busy again?*

"Maybe they're just tired," he said with a shrug. But he still didn't like the fact that something was different.

He rubbed his hand down his stubbly jawline and reached into his pocket, pulling out his cellphone. When he tapped it to life and scrolled to Stella's name, he pressed dial and held it to his ear, waiting. The phone rang out and clicked to her voicemail. He furrowed his brow.

He didn't like this, and the thoughts he had back at the bar came rushing back at him like a tidal wave.

He dialed again, feeling his anger beginning to rise, but this time, Stella answered.

"Hi," she said. Her voice cold and curt.

"Hello..." he said, rubbing his hand through his hair, unsure of what it even was he wanted to say next. "I..." He paused and fell silent. "I just came to Treasured Sweets, but you're not here..." he trailed off.

"We decided to close early," Stella said, but her voice was

so cold that it made him narrow his eyes. She didn't sound like herself, and it was unnerving.

"Okay…" he said, not sure of whether she was being weird with him or not. "I was wondering if you wanted to meet to chat?"

"Chat about what?" she asked.

This was so unlike her, and he knew something was wrong, so he took a breath and cleared his throat.

"Is there something wrong?" he asked. Now, he was beginning to feel really paranoid. On the way to Treasured Sweets, he had tried to convince himself that maybe he had been overthinking, and that, surely, Stella couldn't have been playing him in any way. But hearing her speak so coldly, as if she didn't want him to be calling, was now making his head spin.

"Why don't you tell me," she said, and it stopped him in his tracks.

"What do you mean?" he half-laughed. "You're the one who's being strange, I just called to ask where you were."

"I haven't run off with any dragons, don't worry," she said, and it was so blunt and hurtful that it made him wince.

*What the fuck was going on?*

He gritted his teeth.

"What is that supposed to mean?" he asked her, his voice now echoing hers with annoyance.

"Nothing," she said with a sigh. "Let's just leave it."

But it was too late. He could sense the change in her, and he knew that she must have been speaking to her cousins about what they had said the night before. Now, his head truly was in a mess. He didn't know what he believed anymore.

"What have your cousins been saying?" he asked sternly.

She paused and didn't seem to want to answer.

"I don't really want to get into this, Smith," she said with a sigh. "But let's just say they filled me in on a few things that you didn't seem to be able to last night," she said. "I asked you what they were talking about, and you told me that it wasn't anything to be concerned about, that they would say anything to come between us."

"Yeah," he said, feeling rattled and unsure of how to respond. "So, what exactly have they said?"

She didn't reply, and he could sense that she was getting angry with him again, and he put his hand on the wall outside Treasured Sweets and breathed out deeply. What he wanted to do was rage hell on the dragons, but he was so confused. If only she would open up and speak to him, instead of just instantly siding with them.

"I think you know what they've said," was all Stella came back with.

Smith breathed out again to try to subdue his anger, but it wasn't working. It was rising so high that he felt as if he were about to explode.

"Anyway, I've got to go," she said sadly. "I don't think there's any point in us speaking again until you can be honest about all of this."

And then, before he managed to say another word, the line went dead.

Smith held the phone back from his ear and looked at it, as if he were in disbelief of what had just happened, but also, it was making him even madder. He clearly hadn't overreacted at all. Stella was running rings around him. How could he know if she was truly hurt by the information that he had dated someone who was now seeing one of the dragon clan?

He had never felt so low, and as he turned to walk away, he felt like letting his anger take over and shifting into a bear right there and then. He gritted his teeth and walked forward.

*Those dragons had a lot to answer for.*

# CHAPTER 14

Stella laid in bed and looked up at the ceiling, still feeling as if she had the weight of the world on her shoulders.

She had spent the past few days, since her argument with Smith over the phone, wallowing and not wanting to leave the house. Her aunt had closed up the shop and the stall at the Oktoberfest to come home with her and counsel her after she had found out the information from Dash that Smith had once dated a girl who had left him for a dragon. And it was clear that, even with all of Camille's instant reservations, that she had wanted Stella to try to remain calm.

"Those cousins of yours sure know how to cause trouble," she had said. "They have hearts of gold, and they would do anything for their pack and their family, and also this town… But when it comes to the bears and their rivalry, something just sets them off and makes them act like kids fighting in the school yard. The bears are the same, I've seen it many times over the years, and even though they're all grown men, I can never see it changing."

Stella had pouted and wiped a tear from her eye.

"But why would they drag me into this and make me feel this way if there wasn't good reason?" Stella had asked. "Surely, they wouldn't want to hurt me like that."

"They don't want to hurt you," Camille said. "In their heads, they think they're doing you a favor. They don't know how much Smith means to you already. That you and he have formed a deep connection and bond, for all they knew, the pair of you hadn't even kissed and they were trying to warn you off before you got in too deep. Even if it was partly for their own selfish reasons and to save face within the shifter community."

"Well, they were too late," Stella had said miserably. "And now, I feel worse than ever."

Her aunt had smiled at her sympathetically and rested her hand on top of hers.

"You don't need to keep pushing people away," she had said. "Stella, you deserve to have friends and love and to find happiness. Even if this information is in any way true, it doesn't mean that Smith has anything to be sorry for. It doesn't mean that he targeted you because you're affiliated with his rivals. Why would you think he didn't just fall for you the way you thought?"

Stella had risen from the table and shaken it off. She didn't want to go there. Even if, deep down, she knew her aunt was right. She just couldn't shake the awful feeling that he was going to draw her in and then leave her. It had been her utmost fear since she had lost her parents and she had done a pretty good job, so far, of shunning all serious relationships. But she was so sad, and she missed Smith already. She hated that she had lost control like that, hanging up on Smith and giving him a mouthful. Now, she just wanted to retreat.

So, she had.

And she hadn't left her room since, other than to work

for her aunt before going straight back home. She hadn't seen Smith, he hadn't called her, he hadn't turned up to look for her at Treasured Sweets, and she had avoided everyone in Misty Vale unless they had walked into the store as a customer. She had sat and listened, night after night, to the sound of the festival, and it had made her pine for him even more. And she had kept hearing Camille's words about how she had to stop pushing people away. But she felt as if it were too late, as if she had messed up, and now, there was no turning back. She knew she hadn't cared that Smith had once dated a girl who had left him for a dragon. People get together and break up all the time. But she had let it turn into something much more in her head; she had let it turn into an issue of trust and, in turn, it had panicked her and made her push him away so she didn't have to cope with him potentially leaving her in the future.

She had never been more miserable in her entire life, and now, with the last day of Oktoberfest looming, she didn't know how she was going to carry on in Misty Vale. She had thought, when she'd come back, that she had found a place to call home again. But without Smith and the joy of the festival, she knew it would just feel too empty.

She looked at her empty bags peeking through the crack of the closet door and blinked away a tear.

Maybe it was time to start packing them again, go to Brandon's to collect her car, and get the hell out of this town for good.

It seemed like maybe she wasn't cut out for small-town life after all.

* * *

Brandon's Mechanics was still open when she wandered around after closing up the store on the last night before

Oktoberfest finished. It was a hectic day in town, and people from all over had swarmed into Misty Vale with bright grins and deep pockets, ready to spend their well-earned cash in the shops and stalls that were thriving in the midst of the festivities.

Brandon looked up when she walked toward the main shop door and he paused for a moment, his eyes glossing over her and taking her in.

She smiled and tried not to let her memories of the night in the park overwhelm her. The bears had been so rude, and then, in turn, the next night, so had the dragons. Her Aunt Camille certainly wasn't wrong when she said that their rivalry turned them into silly little kids in the school yard.

"Stella…" Brandon said, as he wiped his oily hands on a rag and shoved it into his back pocket. "How are things?"

"Good, thank you," she said, her tone not entirely convincing. But she didn't owe him anything, and she wasn't about to go into specifics.

"How's my brother doing?" he asked.

She stopped for a moment and felt floored by the question. *Was he joking? Or was he being serious?*

"I don't know," she said, deciding to just straight bat. "You would have to ask him."

Brandon cocked his head to the side quizzically and furrowed his brow, as if she truly had stumped him with her answer and he wanted to ask more but knew that he really shouldn't.

"Anyway," she said. "I'm here for my car… I was wondering if it was finished?"

He nodded his head slowly.

"I was going to call you first thing," he said. "I actually finished it this afternoon."

He wandered farther into the mechanic's shop and toward a small office at the back, with a big glass window that let her see inside. He rummaged around among all of the sets of keys he had on the desk and then swiped hers up and checked them over before rustling through some paperwork.

When he came back out to her, he handed her the keys and the paper that said what he had fixed and why.

"Was it a total mess?" she asked.

"Do you want me to go into it?" he half-laughed.

"Not really, no," she said with a sheepish smile. "It's not like I would have a clue what you're talking about anyway."

Brandon smiled.

"And, of course, there's no charge," he said as if she would likely have been expecting it.

"Huh?" she asked him, her eyes snapping up to meet his.

"No charge," he said. "I want you to know, there's no hard feelings, and Smith and I usually sort things like this out anyway."

She looked at him for a moment, trying to gauge if he was joking or trying to reel her in or something… But he seemed to be being genuine.

"That's not necessary," she said, trying to smile, but her mind was racing, and her nerves were creeping up. "I'll settle it, just write me up an invoice."

Brandon shook his head.

"Stella, it's taken care of," he said reassuringly. "You don't owe me anything."

She stepped back a little and breathed out deeply.

"Really? I mean, I would feel much better if I just settled it myself. I'm going to be leaving town in the morning and I don't want to feel like I'm indebted. I can't imagine I'll find myself back here any time soon."

Now, Brandon looked confused and he put his hands on his hips.

"What would you be leaving for?" he asked. "I thought you'd only just arrived, and things were going good?"

She looked down at the floor and all she could do was shrug.

"I…" She went to speak but had to stop herself because she thought she might cry. "I don't think this place is right for me… And I don't think I'll be missed by anyone. So…"

She held up her keys and said thank you, and then she turned before Brandon could say anything more. After the lecture from Dash, her other cousins, and her aunt, the last thing she needed was some bear trying to coach her on what she should and shouldn't be doing.

When she made it outside, she felt as if the weight of the world was bearing down on her chest and she opened the car door and slipped in behind the wheel. The first thing that sprung to mind was that the last time she had been in this exact spot, she had been steering in the fog and dark while Smith had been pushing the car and helping rescue her. The last time she had been in her car, she had only just met him, and so much had happened since then that it was hard to believe what a crazy couple of weeks it had been.

She closed her eyes and slapped her hand down on the wheel. She couldn't feel any worse, and now, she had the added mystery of why Brandon hadn't seen or spoken to Smith and knew nothing of their fight.

She started the engine and began to back out of the shop, looking up to see Brandon watching her, so she waved meekly before putting the car into drive and getting the hell out of there. She drove out of Main Street, past the festival, and out toward her Aunt Camille's, all the while thinking that as soon as she got there, she was going to throw her things into a bag and let Camille know that she was leaving in the morning. It wasn't going to be easy, but she was going to have to do it for her own sanity.

She pulled up the drive and went into the house. The lights were all on, and Camille was upstairs. Stella snuck up to her room and opened the closet, pulling everything off the racks and shoving them into her bags before she sunk back onto the bed and put her head into her hands.

God, was she miserable and confused…

"Stella?" Camille's voice came from the hallway. "Is that you?"

She looked up and waited for her door to open slightly and Camille smiled as she peeked her head in.

"Yeah," she said sadly.

Camille's eyes went to the bags on the floor and the look of upset etched on Stella's face and she sighed and put her hands on her hips.

"What's going on, sweetheart?" she asked. "Don't tell me you're leaving already?"

Stella nodded slowly, and Camille came in and sat on the edge of the bed.

"If he's making you feel this terrible, then doesn't that show you that he's important?" Camille asked.

The question was heavy and laden with meaning, and she knew what her aunt was trying to say.

"I just can't talk about it anymore…" Stella said. "My mind is working overtime."

Camille nodded with understanding and then she rose to her feet.

"Okay," she said, and Stella could tell that her aunt wasn't going to argue with her. "But there's no way I'm letting you drive out of town tonight when it's already dark. Especially after what happened to you on your way in! Why don't you freshen up and then we can head down for the last night of the festival? I've heard it's going to be the biggest and best finale the town has ever seen."

Stella hesitated and then shook her head. She didn't know about that. What if she got down there and her cousins and the bears were at each other's throats, or she saw Smith and burst into tears?

"I don't know…" she said.

"We can stay out of the way," Camille said, holding out her hand and urging Stella to take it. "Come on, the last thing you need is another night cooped up in this house when there is so much fun to be had out there. And I'm not letting you miss one of the best nights of the year. I would be doing my lovely little town a dis-service.

She thought on it for a moment and could see the hope in her aunt's eyes. She didn't want to hurt her, and she had to admit, it wouldn't be right for her to leave town without spending some quality time with her. Plus, she could even hear the rumble of the music from the Oktoberfest from their house, and she and Camille had been saying they were going to enjoy a night there, and this was their last chance.

"Okay," she said with a smile. "I'll get changed and come downstairs."

"Fantastic," Camille said. "Let's party!"

Stella laughed, and Camille winked.

*I sure am going to miss her…*

# CHAPTER 15

Smith had been moping around his cabin for the best part of a week and he still wasn't feeling like he wanted to deal with anymore shit from his pack. He had managed to work when he'd needed to, and he had kept an eye on the festival from a distance, but now, it was the last night; there was no way he couldn't be down there and in the thick of it.

He had pined for Stella in a way he had never known before. She had haunted his dreams and he had been able to feel her pain too. It was like a physical ache right in his heart, and he had felt all the more miserable for knowing that she was hurting too. He had battled with himself, whether he should call her, and as each day had passed, he had begun to kick himself even more that he hadn't. Now, it felt like it was too late, and he was going to have to resign himself to his fate. He had fucked up and lost her. And now, he would never feel any kind of love like that again.

He pulled on his leather jacket and ran his hand through his hair as he checked his reflection in the mirror before he walked out the door. The night air was crisp and cool, and all the leaves on the oak and sycamore trees were wonderful browns, reds and oranges. When he slipped behind the wheel of his truck and the light lit them up, he smiled, remembering what made this place in the middle of the forest so special, it never faded really. The deciduous trees may shed their leaves, but they were still flanked by the pines, and they stayed thick and lush for him all year long. It reminded him of something, but he couldn't grasp the memory, until, suddenly, it hit him like a slap in the face. The trees were reminding him of his night of passion in the forest with Stella out the back of the festival, and now, he felt the ache all over again.

When he arrived at Oktoberfest, he parked his truck outside the park and walked in through the main gates with the heavy throngs of people who were also just arriving for the last night of celebrations. The stalls were all open and packed, the scent of baking and beer filled the air, along with smoke from the firepits and the sound of yodeling coming from a competition that had been set up on the main stage.

As he passed by Treasured Sweets stall, he couldn't help but look, and he was surprised to see that it was open, but neither Stella nor Camille were the ones running it. It looked to be one of Camille's Saturday girls, and he felt a knot of guilt in his stomach. He wondered if they were still at home and what was happening, or if they were even in town or had left to escape the last night of partying. His mind began to turn over as he reached the main space, and the teepee was suddenly overhead. He looked around and it wasn't long before he recognized his bear brothers and the pitch they had set up ahead of the stage, they were all watching the yodelers and were cheering, clapping and laughing.

"Smith." He heard the voice come from the crowd behind him and he turned to see Brandon coming toward him with a large mug of ale and a look of concern. "What's happening, man? Where have you been?"

Smith shrugged his shoulders and then looked up.

"Oh, you know, just this and that, here and there," he said. "I've had quite a bit to catch up on and didn't want to get all swept up in this each night too. You know what it's like when we all get together and start drinking..." He laughed, and Brandon nodded his head slowly.

"Have you seen Stella?" he asked, and this certainly got Smith's attention.

Smith's eyes focused in on Brandon's and he watched him for a moment, waiting to see if he spoke again.

"No," he finally had to answer. "Why? Did she call about her car?"

"No," Brandon said. "She came and got it."

Smith nodded his head slowly.

"She just turned up earlier, and I asked her how you were doing, and she seemed a little rattled by it. She said I'd have to ask you."

"Well, isn't that something..." Smith said with a raised brow.

He wanted to turn away from Brandon and forget this whole conversation, but Brandon ducked in front of him again and blocked his path.

"She took the car and said something else," Brandon said ominously.

Now, he was testing Smith's patience and he found himself glaring at him.

"Oh really? Well, what did she say?" he asked, finally giving Brandon what he wanted.

"She told me she was leaving town," Brandon said, and he looked worried. Smith could tell he took no pleasure in saying it.

"What do you mean?" he asked.

"She said she was packing up and leaving, that she wasn't cut out for it here and it wasn't what she thought it would be. She also said she didn't think she would be missed by anyone."

The words hit Smith like a truck. He didn't know why, but he had not been expecting that. Stella had just come back to Misty Vale, and he had thought there would be time… Time for him to think, time for him to do something, time for him to make it up to her… And now, it seemed like it was all about to be ripped away.

"I know I had to let you know as soon as possible," Brandon said sympathetically. "And also, I wanted to say I'm sorry for all that happened out in the park the other night. We were all wasted, you know we just want what is best for you."

Smith's eyes flicked up to meet his and he felt grateful for Brandon's apology.

"We had no right to act that way," Brandon continued. "All of us have spoken about it and it was just so silly and out of hand. You know what those dragons do to us. But Stella isn't a dragon, you're right. It's not her fault that she was born into that family. And not only that…" he continued. "But I've seen the change in you. I know I haven't found my mate yet, but we all said that we recognized it in you and Stella. You guys have something. Something real and impor-tant, and we never should have tried to get in the way of that. You can't fight it, Smith. You need to go after her before it's too late."

Smith felt spurred into action and he felt like kissing Brandon. He had been wondering what the hell he could do and what on Earth he was going to say, but he didn't need to think it over anymore. The thought of Stella feeling so low that she was about to leave town was like a knife to the heart, and he was so grateful to Brandon for finding him and telling him while he still had a chance.

*Well, I hope I still have a chance.*

"What time did she come and collect her car?" he asked Brandon with panic.

"Around six," he said. "She said she was leaving town tomorrow."

Smith looked at his watch and it was almost nine." He ran his hands through his hair and tried to think fast. Where the hell should he go to find her? The obvious place was her aunt's, but what if they weren't home?

He was about to dash back to his truck when Brandon nudged him and motioned in the direction of the beer tents. On a table, sitting with a blanket slung over her knee and being warmed by a firepit, she saw Stella and Camille, sitting together, watching the yodelers and sharing a bottle of red wine.

His heart came alive all over again. She looked so radiant, but he could still see the sadness behind her eyes, and he couldn't believe that he had been the cause of it.

He looked at her, and then he looked at the crowd, and then to the stage. The yodeling competition was about to finish and he knew exactly what he had to do.

He had to get up there and show her exactly how much she meant to him.

# CHAPTER 16

Stella was being warmed by the fire raging next to her in the pit, and the lovely fur blanket that she had over her knees. The wine she and Camille had chosen was smooth and full-bodied, and as it rolled over her tongue and went down her throat, it felt like velvet. It was helping her unwind and relax after what had been a very stressful few days, and it was most needed.

The yodeling competition had been hilarious to watch, and had lifted her mood slightly, but she had the overwhelming feeling that Smith was nearby, and it was making her nervous. She felt the tug of him, as if his soul had found hers in the atmosphere, and he was pulling her to him, winding her up into his heart, and she had to resist it. Even if she didn't want to. She took another sip of wine and looked ahead at the stage. The competition had come to a close and the winner was being crowned. It was a local lady her aunt seemed to know.

"I'm glad someone from Misty Vale won this year," Camille said. "Usually, it is one of the tourists. That is one of the reasons they love to come out here to the festival, because they get to show off their skills. No one from our town has ever won it before," she laughed. "But by the looks of it, Mary had been practicing and taking lessons. I had no idea she could belt out sounds like that."

"It was certainly very impressive," Stella agreed. She had never witnessed a yodeling competition before, so she hadn't known what to expect, but it hadn't disappointed. It had been hilarious to watch so many people get up on stage and try their hand at the Alpine European tradition. Even though many of them were terrible, and a lot of them were drunk, some of the contestants genuinely had a talent for it, and it had certainly been great entertainment for the last night of the festival. The only other act on the agenda, now, was the closing band who was due to begin at ten and then carry on until the early hours, finishing off Misty Vale's Oktoberfest for another year and signaling the end of fall and the beginning of the longer winter nights.

Stella looked over to her aunt and smiled. She really did love it here now, and it was such a shame that she was feeling like she had to run again. She had come back with such low expectations, just the need to be closer to her only family and maybe try to settle and put down some permanent roots. But she had quickly started to fall for this place, to see its charm, and she loved working in Treasured Sweets. The thought of heading back to a cold and isolating city, where she would be, once again, looking for an apartment share and a new job had seemed the only option over the past few days, but the more she thought about it, the more it made her sad.

She sighed and took another sip of wine. She was going to need a lot of it to get through how tough the next few hours were going to be. She didn't want to tell Camille that she wanted to go back to the house, and she didn't want to cut their last night together short either. But she was feeling weary, and the sensation that Smith was close to her was beginning to make her skin tingle. She hadn't felt it since their fight, as if he had purposely avoided her, as she had him, but right there in the mix of all those people, she could feel him strongly and she knew he had to be there.

It wasn't until she heard the crowd begin to quieten and the lights flashed onto the stage that the feeling became more intense. She was aware of something happening up there, and she saw the look of shock on her aunt's face as she looked ahead and stared at the stage, her mouth gaping slightly open.

"What is it?" Stella asked.

Her aunt didn't respond, but Stella followed her eyeline and it took her to the stage, where, standing there, holding the microphone and waiting for everyone's attention, was Smith.

Her heart seemed to clang in her chest, and she felt herself sit up straighter. She hadn't been expecting to see him right there, and it made her heart race, and her palms go slick with nervous sweat. She swallowed and blinked, just to make sure she wasn't imagining anything. But he was still standing there, looking back at the crowd, before he tapped the end of the microphone and held it up to his lips.

"Good evening, everyone," Smith said, his voice echoing out around the teepee and the surrounding areas. The speakers were turned up so high that it would be a miracle if the whole of Misty Vale didn't hear him.

The crowd was now silent, and more and more people gathered, looking up at him on the stage, standing there looking so fucking sexy that it made Stella's bones ache.

*But what was he doing? Why was he even up there?*

"Thank you for your attention," he said, his voice calm

and collected. "I think we can all agree that what we saw just now, with the yodeling, was one of the finest displays of powerful lungs this town has ever seen."

The crowd began to laugh and clap, their cheers rang out around the park before they became hushed again and their attention went back to Smith.

"That is what Oktoberfest is all about; it's about having fun, losing your inhibitions, and celebrating with people. It's what our town is about too… Here, in Misty Vale, we all come together and show our love for one another by having fun and trying to spread that joy out to the rest of the world."

The crowd cheered and clapped again, and Stella felt a tear welling up behind her eye. She felt fixed to the spot, but it felt so hard to watch him up there, giving this speech.

"Normally, my brother does the closing speech, but tonight, I had to get up here because I wanted to speak about something that is very important to me. Not only do I want to thank each and every one of you that has traveled here to our little town and supported us, but also to our community for coming together and throwing the best Oktoberfest we have ever seen. It truly has been something remarkable."

The crowd roared, and Smith clapped too, his warm smile spreading out across the park. Stella felt a pang of longing.

"You see, only a couple of weeks ago, I thought I didn't want to be a part of this place anymore…"

The crowd fell silent and a low hush of disapproval rumbled lowly through the crowds. Stella frowned, and looked across at Camille, before she stared back up at Smith.

"I was disillusioned with everything… With my work, my family, my place in life here in general…" he continued. "I was even on my way out of here, with no intention of coming back. But then, something happened. I think a lot of people would call it a miracle, or maybe fate…"

He turned now and stared straight at Stella. Her heart thumped in her chest and her mouth dropped open. His eyes were fixed directly on hers and she felt him all over her. She felt his touch, his soul, his heart… She took him in and, for a moment, they could have been the only two people in the world.

"While I was leaving town, I met someone."

Smith's words were huge, but they were directed only at her. The whole town was there watching, and they followed his stare to Stella, and, suddenly, a small spotlight from the back of the stage spun and landed on her, lighting her up for all to see.

She felt frozen, but she didn't want to sit there looking like a deer caught in the headlights, so she rose to her feet and smiled.

"I met you, Stella," Smith said, his words now only for her. "And you changed everything."

She felt the tears welling up behind her eyes and she wrapped her arms around herself, unsure of what else she could do.

"You brought me back here by chance, but you also brought me back here by fate… Because the second I met you out there on the mountain, I knew. I knew I had found the person I was supposed to spend the rest of my life with. And it doesn't matter how many challenges are thrown our way, how many times our families may collide, we know what our love is. It's real and it's true… And I do, Stella, I really do… I love you. I love you with all my heart."

The crowd began to cheer, and Smith smiled as he began to walk down the steps of the stage, heading toward her. The crowd parted to let him through, and Stella beamed at him.

She had no idea what was happening, but it felt so right. She couldn't believe he had gotten up there, that he had publicly declared his love for her. And now, he was right there in front of her, holding out his arms. She rushed into them and looked into his eyes as the whole of Misty Vale cheered for them. The energy was electric, and she felt it deep in her bones. She looked up at Smith, at the man who had become everything to her, and he cupped her face. She saw the bear in him, and she knew she loved him too. More than she had ever loved anyone or anything. And to be there with him in this town was an honor. She didn't want to leave; she had never wanted to leave. She wanted to be there with him, and when the prospect of that had been taken away, it had been her instinct to run. But he had saved her. He really had. And now, he had done this in front of both their families, and they all knew what they meant to one another.

"I love you too, Smith," she whispered, so the words were just for them.

Smith leaned in and kissed her, taking her breath away, as the whole crowd roared and cheered. They clapped for them and their love, and now, the whole world knew, their families knew, that whatever happened, they would not be broken. The moment could not have been any more perfect, and when their lips came apart and they looked into each other's eyes again, Stella wrapped her arms around his neck and shoulders and nuzzled into his chest.

*This is where I belong, with Smith, in Misty Vale. My home.*

When the crowd had started to go back to normal and people were beginning to dance to the band as they came on stage, Stella still couldn't believe what Smith had done, and what he had confessed. She had no idea he was leaving town the night they met, and now, he had stopped her from going too. It was like a full-circle moment that unified their love even more.

Stella was aware of the eyes of her cousins on her from somewhere in the crowd and when she turned to look at them and caught their eye, she saw Dash and Striker tip their heads and smile. She looked back to Smith, who was watching them too, and to her delight, she saw them smile and acknowledge him too. Stella nodded, showing them that she appreciated what they had done, and Striker, Dash, and Zane all did too. They didn't have to say anything, but they all knew.

It may not have been a major truce, but it was certainly headway, and she could see that they were going to be accepting of them from now on, and that they wouldn't be trying to make her doubt their love. She knew her cousins had meant well, and they clearly hadn't known how serious Smith and Stella had felt about each other, but now that he had gotten up in front of the whole town and basically told them she was his fated mate, there was no turning back. Shifters didn't interfere with things like that, and it was down to them, now, to respect their union.

"Well, you two…" Camille said as she joined them and put her hand on Smith's shoulder. "I think we can safely say that was one hell of an ending to this year's Oktoberfest."

"It sure was." Stella beamed as she looked up at Smith and leaned into him again.

"I'm going to get myself home," she said. "I've had enough excitement to see me through until Christmas now…"

Stella kissed her aunt goodbye, and she watched as she reached up and touched Smith affectionately on the cheek. She didn't say a word, but she didn't have to, and as she walked off, and they were left alone, Stella knew what she wanted to do more than anything.

"I think we should head home too," she said mischievously.

"You're damned right, we should," Smith said with a low growl, as he reached down and swept her up in his arms and began to carry her, through the crowd, to his truck. The crowd cheered behind them as they made their way through, as if he were carrying her over the threshold. She wrapped her arms around his neck and breathed him in.

What a night it had been. And what a perfect way to end the festival. Misty Vale was shining bright.

# CHAPTER 17

$S$tella watched as Smith lit the candles around the bedroom, a fire already blazing in the corner of the room, casting out orange light and making it feel so cozy and warm. It felt so romantic, as if she had stepped into a movie, and when he turned and looked at her, she felt her heart pound and her nerves rise.

It was hot in there, and she was responding to it. She laid there, her whole body alive and full of want as his eyes moved over her, undressing her slowly with each passing second.

He had removed his jacket and thrown it down on the bed next to her, and when he stepped toward her, she felt her nipples harden. She had waited for this moment since the second she had laid eyes on him. The night they had frolicked in the woods together and made each other come so hard had only teased her for more, and she knew she couldn't wait any longer.

She wanted him to do this. She wanted him to claim her.

She knew the consequences and what it would mean, and

she couldn't think of any other way now. She was Smith's woman. He had found her in this crazy world, and they had fallen for each other. A shifter knows when his one true mate arrives, and as he had said tonight, Stella was it.

She leaned back on her elbows and looked up at him, as he pulled his t-shirt off over his head, exposing his incredible muscles. He looked so damned good, and as the flames from the fire danced around the darkened room, they lit up his abs and made them look even deeper, carved and stronger. It made her breathless and want him even more.

Smith looked down at her with a wry smile and he began to pull her jeans down slowly, teasing them off the ends of her feet and throwing them onto the floor behind him. Stella panted as he reached for his own belt buckle, snapping it open and pulling it out of the loops before throwing it onto the floor. She sat forward and he lifted her top up over her head, snapping off her bra with his free hand and exposing her ample breasts. He groaned when he saw them, reached down and cupping them, biting his lip and adjusting his cock through his pants.

"You've got me so hard," he said breathlessly.

Stella looked up into his eyes and laid back on the bed, only wearing her panties. Smith hooked his fingers into the corners of them, easing them down and throwing them over his shoulder, before he pulled down his jeans and underwear, exposing himself, showing her the full extent of him. She had felt him before, she had made him come, but seeing him there in front of him like that made her pussy so wet and engorged that she could barely stand it.

*Finally.*

She was beyond ready for him. She gasped as Smith kneeled on the bed in front of her and parted her legs. He pulled her forward, so her butt was resting right on the edge and he looked deep into her eyes. She could barely breathe; the anticipation was so much.

As Smith reached down between her legs and dipped a finger into her pussy, he groaned when he felt how wet she was for him. He slicked some of her juices onto his hand and massaged her clit, and she threw back her head as a warm wave of pleasure rolled over her.

"Yes," she gasped as he worked at her.

She bucked her hips up to meet his hand, and he pushed her back down, pulling his hand away and smirking at her. Making her wait.

She sat up and pulled him to her, taking his cock in her mouth and right to the back of her throat. As she sucked him, he moaned and held her head, telling her yes and moving his hips forward, fucking her mouth slowly, tensing his thighs.

When he reached down and cupped her breasts, she could taste him, salty and ready on her tongue, and she couldn't hold on any longer. She laid back, and Smith climbed between her thighs, taking tight hold of his huge engorged cock with one hand and pinning her down with the other.

He put his weight on her, and when she felt him penetrate her, she gasped and opened herself as wide as she could. He went so deep inside of her, sending the most intense wave of pleasure rocketing through her that she reached up to grip the bedsheet and screamed up to the ceiling.

*Yes! Claim me! Take me...*

As his thrusts became more powerful and intense and she felt the bear in him rise to the surface, she wrapped her legs around him and felt tiny in his arms. His cock was so big and powerful, with each buck of his hips, it felt as if he were finding new places inside of her that had never been touched before. She was so wet for him, and he was so hard, and when she felt him work up to his release, she gripped the sheets again and began to unravel beneath him. Her pleasure began to send him into a frenzy, and he held his head back and roared as he spilled his seed inside of her and claimed her as his own.

The bear had claimed his fated mate, and as they both laid there basking in the aftermath of their love, Stella had never felt so hot or alive. The pleasure rocketed through her, leaving her trembling, and Smith grunted and growled as his own release jerked out of him, the bear taking her and his energy merging with hers for all time.

When he crashed down onto the mattress next to her and pulled her as close to him as he could get her, their bodies were sticky and slick with sweat. The room raged with the orange glow of the fire, and she felt forever changed. Her vision felt clearer and her senses were heightened, her orgasm was still lingering, and it felt more intense, her pussy still throbbing and feeling so good.

"Wow," she panted. Unable to say anything more.

Smith wrapped his hand up in her hair and kissed her on the forehead. Both of them still breathless and unable to speak.

She couldn't believe how different she felt, but it was so right. It almost felt as if she always should have been this way, and as she felt his energy course through her veins, she knew she truly had never been part of the dragon family at all.

*I was always meant to be a bear.*

She nuzzled into him as they basked in the glow of each other, and Smith cradled her. She was his fated mate, and he was her bear. They were joined together for all time, by body, heart and soul… And now, there was truly no going back.

They may have both been about to leave Misty Vale behind for good but finding each other had brought them back to where they truly belonged, and now, Stella and Smith had found their one true family.

Together, they were ready to take on anything. And they were both finally home.

# CHAPTER 18

*One Month Later*

The moon was big and full in the night sky, shining out of the inky blackness and lighting up the forest paths that led out of the cabin and into the woodland.

Stella stood up on the veranda with a blanket wrapped around her shoulders and a mug of hot cocoa in her palms, blowing the steam from it and taking little sips to help warm her through. Winter had now fully arrived in Misty Vale and the first snow had started to fall. As she stood out back and looked up at the moon and the heavens, she saw the true beauty of this place. The majestic nature of the pine trees and of how they protected Smith and his secret world. The bears and dragons of this town had hidden for generations, and only those truly in the know had any real idea. No matter how many rumors may swirl around, from time to time, through the high school kids and the odd TV show on the paranormal, no one except the trusted truly knew. To be fully on the inside was humbling, and Stella knew how virtuous and true the shifter packs of Misty Vale were, even if they still had their problems with each other.

Smith came out the doors behind her and wrapped his arms around her waist before he kissed the side of her neck. She swooned into him. Feeling the tense nature of their passion rising. Since he had claimed her, they could barely even touch each other without wanting to rip each other's clothes off, and they both knew it was only a matter of time before they heard the tiny pitter patter of bear cub feet.

She smiled and turned her head to the side as he rested his chin on her shoulder.

"What a moon," he said as he looked up at it longingly.

"It's a beautiful night," she agreed.

"A fine night for shifting," the voice came from behind them and Brandon came walking around the side of the cabin with a big smirk on his face.

Smith and Stella laughed, and it was clear that Smith couldn't agree more.

He kissed Stella on the cheek and jumped over the side of the veranda, landing down on the frozen earth next to Brandon and clasping his fist before they hugged and slapped each other on the back.

"Are we going up top?" Brandon asked as he cast his eyes toward the mountains.

"Fuck yeah," Smith grinned. "Stella is going to watch us."

She raised her eyebrows in a wiggle and grinned.

"Have fun, boys," she said as Smith looked up at her longingly and smiled.

They could look at each other now and know what the other was thinking and his eyes were telling her that he adored her, and once he got home, he was going to strip her bare and make love to her again and again. She bit her lip and grinned. She loved it when he came home full of his bear energy, especially after he had been up on the mountain to shift.

Brandon and Smith wandered closer to the forest edge,

and while Brandon went into the privacy of the pine trees, Smith stood in full view of Stella as he began to change. His clothes ripped off his back and his growls and groans became louder as his skin split open and the dark black fur sprung up in its place. His bear was so big and powerful, and to know it was inside of him at all times turned Stella on so much that she could barely hold it together when she saw him this way. It was scary but also exhilarating.

The bear looked back at her and growled out a roar so loud it made her shudder and narrow her eyes. She could feel the power hurtling toward her, and she knew that when Smith was back in human form, she was in for one hell of a night.

As the bear ducked into the forest, she raised her hand, waved and watched as he disappeared. The padding of their paws became lighter and fainter the farther away they went, but she saw the trees moving as they passed them by, and she knew they were heading up to the mountain.

She sipped her cocoa and smiled. *This is everything I never knew I needed.* She was totally taken by the sheer bliss of the moment...

The snow-capped mountains were spread out ahead of her, and when she looked at them now, she couldn't believe that she had ever left this place behind. It was home, and it always would be. She thought, when she had lost her family, that this place was alien to her and that it would always remind her of that. But it turned out that Misty Vale had brought her family back to her, their memory lived on in the stars above her, and Smith was her family now. The man she would live and grow with until they were old and gray. Her parents would have loved him, she was sure of that. And she smiled when she looked up at the stars and saw two bright ones shining down. She looked at them each night and spoke to them, knowing they were watching over her.

She smiled and felt warmth spread through her. Love was all around her, with Smith, with her aunt, with both her dragon and bear families, and now, with the spirit of her parents in the heavens above her. Misty Vale had it all, and she was indebted to this place for the rest of time.

Stella had finally found a place in the world to call her own, a man to love, and a life to look forward to.

*Fate always finds a way.*

* * *

THANK YOU SO MUCH FOR READING SAVAGE BEAR'S FATED Mate! If you loved this we are sure you will want to catch up on all the previous series, now available in one giant Box Set!

Get the 3 Box set collection, Bad Boy Shifter Love HERE on Amazon…

If you are all caught up then check out the first book in Samantha and Pamela Avery's new Mossy Ridge series…

Here is a short preview…

"WELL, SHIT," MONICA WHISPERED TO HERSELF AS SHE PULLED into the driveway. Her chestnut waves fell into her face as she looked at her house. She absolutely loved this place. Her brother, Frank, was sitting on the porch with a sheepish expression. He always looked that way. He was the best. Her brother gave her faith that there were good men out there, after all was said and done.

"Hey, Frank, whatcha doing here?" she said aloud, with a smile.

He gave her a sly smile, "Brought the kids a pack of smokes and a beer, Monnie, what else am I good for?"

Monica snorted. "Get outta here, Frank. You're not allowed in any liquor store for fifty miles." He snorted back, the same snort; because it was one of the many things they had in common. He was her safest and best friend. She sat down beside him on the steps, leaned over, and rested her head on his shoulder. Their matching chestnut hair, side-by-side, made it look like an ad for autumn. "Man, today was long, Frank. Is there anything up or are you just here to cheer me up?"

Frank reached around her shoulders and gave her a squeeze. "Well, I've got a problem with a bank loan. I think I have it figured out, but it isn't for today. Today, I'm just here to say hey… and I fed the kids some supper from the freezer. Hope you don't mind. I'm sorry if that was overstepping."

The voices of two kids overlapped each other as they yelled from the house, "It was disgusting, Mom! Pizza! From the *freezer*" one voice said.

"I'm never talking to Uncle Frank *again*! He made me use a *napkin*!!" said the other.

The comments were followed by barks and laughs of the pre-teen sort, fading as the boys moved away from the windows. Frank laughed and called into the house, smiling, "You punks better be cleaning up in there, or I'll block you from the Hut!" Groans and snorts came in reply.

Monica stared at him and choked back a sob. "*Oh my God*, Frank, I was dreading even thinking about dinner. Thank you *so* much! It's the most thoughtful and concretely helpful thing you could possibly have done. You just gave me a whole night. A whole night!" It was astonishing how fast her emotions flew when she was home. Who was she kidding? They flew everywhere, all the time lately!! Her deep green eyes were full of tears already, damn it. She couldn't believe how close her emotions were to the edge today!

She always thought she had it so together, and someone does *one* nice thing and all her work in keeping up the façade of 'having it all together' just exploded into pieces. She did her best to push her fears away, just about every day. She looked at him in tears, smiling slightly, "And don't think I won't find out more about the bank loan. It will just have to wait 'til I'm done with my breakdown..." Frank smiled down at her.

Sigh. There were some days it was just all too fucking much.

Ugh, she chastised her inner sailor for all the swearing. It was a joke with Frank and the kids, and all of her oldest and best friends. Nobody would ever guess what a foul mouth she had. She could completely hide it. It never showed at the office, the PTO, the Town Council, ever. Not even when the situation completely called for it. If you could stick a microphone in someone's mind, hers would be the most profane ever heard. A lot of times, it made her laugh; it felt more authentic somehow. It had taken a lot of therapy to get to this point, but she accepted it. Her pint-sized body contained a six-foot salty-mouthed sailor, and she couldn't seem to fix it. She rolled her eyes at herself and looked over at her brother.

Monica blinked hard several times, to try and clear her mind of the criticisms of the past. She grinned at Frank. She had no idea how he ran an entertainment center for kids. But he did, and he did it well. The Bouncy Hut was a raging success, according to everyone, but only she knew how much he had overcome to make it a success. She was so proud of him.

In many ways, The Bouncy Hut felt like the center of town, at least for her. Her kids spent all their spare time there, and Frank was actually a quiet father figure to a lot of the kids in town. He'd managed to learn a different way, somehow, from how they'd been raised. It was nothing short of miraculous. The way he loved her boys blew her heart wide open.

It had been a long day, but look, she had an entire evening free of chores and hustle. It was a miracle! She and the kids could just tuck in and watch a movie or maybe she'd even drag out the board games she kept buying in hopes they'd eventually do a 'game night'. *Oh my god, that was it.*

"Frank, come on in. I think we're doing game night. We'd love a fourth...whaddaya say? It'll only take a few hours off your life...I think today's game might be Monopoly. You know you're the best at the money. Wink, wink." she said in a wheedling voice. She backed into the door of the house, waving him in.

Frank laughed, "Oh God, this is going to be horrible..."


Get Enemy Daddy Bear HERE on Amazon...

www.ingramcontent.com/pod-product-compliance
Lightning Source LLC
Chambersburg PA
CBHW051426150726
48000CB00005B/1978